Enjoy this
tundra
adventure!

Laurie JWood

Jude 1:24

NORTHERN DECEPTION

HEROES OF THE TUNDRA, BOOK 1

LAURIE WOOD

Books that Inspire!

NORTHERN DECEPTION
Heroes of the Tundra, Book 1
By Laurie Wood
© Copyright 2021 Laurie Wood

Published by Anaiah Edge
An imprint of Anaiah Press, LLC.
7780 49th ST N. #129
Pinellas Park, FL 33781

Second Anaiah Edge ebook edition January 2022
Book Cover and Interior Design by Eden Plantz

For Paul, my real-life hero who's gone through the fire, and come back again.

ACKNOWLEDGMENTS

Many people contribute their help with writing a book, and this book was no exception. For the technical research, I sincerely thank the following people:

Stephen D. Petersen, Head, Conservation and Research, Assiniboine Park Zoo—Assiniboine Park Conservancy, Winnipeg, Manitoba, for his answers regarding polar bear satellite research projects and their life in the wild.

John Gunter, President and CEO of Frontiers North, Churchill, Manitoba, for discussing his trademarked Tundra Buggies, which I turned into "Arctic Rovers" as a fictionalized version of his superior tourist vehicles, as well as a few stories about the town.

Jessica Hunt, Executive Assistant of the Town of Churchill, Manitoba, for answering many questions by phone, and never getting tired of hearing from me. You rock! And if we are ever in town, I owe you at least lunch.

And to Kara Leigh Miller, Editorial Director of Anaiah Press, thank you so much for seeing the promise in this book and championing it! Because of you, the Canadian north is going to enjoy a whole new audience.

Julie Sturgeon, my editor, many thanks for helping me shine up my prose and walking me through the process.

And to Tina Radcliffe, author, who saw something in me and nurtured my belief in myself two years ago—I can't thank you enough!

My Writing Sisters—you all know who you are—here's to the best yet to come.

ABOUT THE AUTHOR

Laurie Wood is a military wife who's lived across Canada and visited six of its ten provinces. She and her husband have raised two wonderful children with Down Syndrome to adulthood, and their son and daughter are a wonderful blessing to their lives. Over the years, Laurie's books have finaled in prestigious contests such as the Daphne du Maurier (twice), the TARA, the Jasmine, and the Genesis. Her family lives in central Canada with a menagerie of rescue dogs and cats. If the house were bigger, no doubt they'd have more.

Website: https://www.lauriewoodauthor.com
Facebook: https://www.facebook.com/lauriewoodauthor
Twitter: https://twitter.com/LaurieJeanWood

Place me like a seal over your heart,
Like a seal on your arm;
For love is as strong as death,
Its jealousy as unyielding as the grave.

Song of Songs 8:6

CHAPTER 1

Kira Summers shivered as she stood beside her brother's open grave. Winnipeg Memorial Cemetery stood bleak and empty. The November sky churned with rain clouds as purple as bruises.

Her fingers trembled on the handle of her black umbrella. Sleety snow swirled across the grass and lashed around the ankles of her short dress boots. Kira's pulse roared in her ears, and for a split second, she swayed, feeling light-headed. She stifled her sobs with a tissue.

"I'm sorry I'm late."

"Oh," she gasped. Her heart thrummed against her chest. She didn't need to turn around to know who was behind her.

"How long have you been standing there?" She jammed the tissue into her pocket.

"I just got here." His hand grasped her elbow and gently turned her around. She looked up into ice-blue eyes she'd never forgotten. "Kira, I'm so, so sorry Michael's gone."

She raised an eyebrow at his hand on her elbow. He let her go and thrust his hands into the front pockets of his jeans, rocking back and forth on his heels.

Here he was, Lukas Tanner, her long-lost love and the last man she expected to see today. Or any day, for that matter. She tried to force a smile and failed. "How did you find out?"

"The world's a small place." He shrugged. "We've still got newspapers up north. I saw his obituary."

She huffed as she turned away and blew her nose. "I meant, how did you know I was here? At the cemetery?"

He took the umbrella from her and placed his hand again on her elbow, turning her away from the flower-drenched coffin. "Where else would you be? And where's Aunt June?"

"Her arthritis is acting up. The rain. She didn't want to leave but..." Kira paused. "She did most of the funeral arrangements."

Lukas filled the space she hadn't realized felt like a gaping hole. She had company now. Someone who *knew* her down to her soul. He stared into her eyes, with the space between them crackling like lightening in a hot summer sky.

"I'm sorry. My flight was delayed, or I would've met you at the church."

She stiffened. Her throat worked at trying not to cry again. She didn't want to leave her brother, Michael, her only blood relative. He would be all alone, buried in this lonely place. She didn't live in Winnipeg anymore. She'd left for a job and run away. Run away from the man who now stood beside her on the frozen grass.

"You're freezing. Let's get you someplace warm." His hand on the small of her back guided her to the black rental car he'd parked behind hers. "Is there anywhere in particular you want to go?"

She snatched the umbrella back. "Everything I need is in the car. I'm flying back to Churchill now. I'm sorry you came all this way for nothing."

She resisted the urge to reach out and touch him. He wasn't dressed for a funeral or the weather. A worn, brown bomber jacket covered a red plaid shirt. He stood as solid and reassuring as she remembered: his hands shoved again into his front jean pockets like he always had. Sun-bleached highlights rimmed his hair. "He was the brother I never had." Those arctic-blue eyes pierced her heart. "How

2

could I not come?" The left side of his mouth still quirked up when he was nervous.

Kira clutched the neck of her jacket tighter against the sleet sweeping across the manicured grounds. He'd come. Lukas and Michael had grown up together, inseparable and always in trouble when they were young. Then there was her and Lukas. She pressed her lips together. Those thoughts led to pain.

"I need to get to the airport."

"I want to know how he died in a car accident. He was a great driver."

Tears threatened to spill over again. She looked away. "It was a rollover on the Perimeter highway. He must've been going too fast that afternoon. The police said he rolled twice." Her cheeks were numb. "The ditch had water in it, they said." Her voice cracked. "He drowned in a couple inches of water."

Kira could see Lukas's throat muscles working. Pain contorted his face.

"I have to go. I'm late," she said. If she stood in front of him a second longer, she'd fall apart. She didn't owe him anything. Kira turned away and headed up to her own car.

"I'll meet you at the airport." His voice fell away behind her.

Kira tossed her purse and umbrella into the car and swung her legs in beneath the wheel. Plastic totes filled with Michael's books and memorabilia filled the back seat of the small sedan. Her luggage was in the trunk. She'd be paying a pretty penny in freight charges to fly everything home to Churchill.

A van screeched up beside her driver's door, sliding sideways onto the grass as it came to a stop. She glimpsed a male driver with sunglasses and a ball cap just before her door was thrown open by another man.

"Out, out, out!"

The man wore a navy blue ski mask. He grabbed her by the shoulders and hauled her halfway out of the car. Muscle memory allowed her to shove her right palm hard against his nose. It gave a satisfying crunch even as he pulled her from the safety of the driver's seat. He clasped her arms like a vise, but she kicked hard and felt the solid heels of her boots connecting with his shins.

With a yell, her captor let go of her arms, and she fell to the pavement on her left side, rolling towards the open door of the van. Lukas grabbed the man from behind while tightening his right arm across the man's throat.

"Come on!" The driver pounded his fist on the sliding van door.

"Lukas, you'll kill him!"

Lukas shoved her attacker away from him. The guy leapt into the open side door of the van. The driver peeled away with the other man cursing as he struggled to hold on to the van's door.

Kira pushed herself up from the pavement. Her tights were in shreds, and her hair had come undone from its bun. Panting, she stumbled upright. Lukas grasped her shoulders.

"Stupid question, but are you okay?"

What was that? It was like walking into her college dorm room and feeling the knife shoved against her throat by the man in black. *No, no, not again. Dear Lord, protect me...*

She wavered on her feet and drew in a shaky breath. "Sure, yeah—no, no I'm not!"

He pulled her against his chest. "Just take another breath."

Adrenaline surged through her body, electrifying her blood vessels. Her legs wobbled like a newborn foal. She refused to give in to the warmth and the delicious scent of his leather jacket, even as her cheek registered the soft flannel shirt poking out from the open zipper. Where were his pressed and preppy clothes? His heart pounded too; she could feel his pulse beating at the base of his throat.

"Who were those guys?" The deep timbre of his voice rumbled against her hair.

She clutched the edges of his jacket. "No idea." Her boots raised her to underneath his chin. "Now I'm really late." She tilted her head back enough to look at him. "Thank you."

Now it was his turn to huff out a breath. "Thank you? You were nearly dragged off—we've got to call the police."

"No, I'll miss my flight." She pushed away from his chest. Call the police? They hadn't bothered to help her five years ago when she reported the vicious assault on her in her dorm room. She despised the police. Why would they believe her this time?

"Kira. We have to report this. I'll go with you."

She shook her head and hefted her purse onto her shoulder.

"At least make a phone call."

I'll miss my flight. I'll miss my flight, echoed in her head. Great. She was losing her mind. Her stomach roiled. No way was she going to pass out, throw up, or fall into his arms.

"I'll call from the airport. I gotta go." With unsteady steps, Kira picked her way across the gravel driveway and made it to the car door.

"Kira," Lukas shouted behind her.

Escape... run away... it was what she did best. She fired up the engine, slammed the door, and raised a hand to wave at him in the back mirror. Then she squealed her tires away from the side of the cemetery driveway and left him standing in her dust.

Lukas gave up on flipping through the travel magazines from the back pocket of the airplane seat in front of him. Kira sat two rows ahead of him, although on the twenty-two seat Calm airplane, they were almost the only people on board. He could see the back of her head. She'd scraped her hair back into a severe bun. When it had hung in waves about her face after the attempted kidnapping, he'd noticed bright streaks of teal underneath, which belied her cool, detached scientist demeanor. She'd always been a wild child until everything changed in university. He still didn't know why.

He'd scrutinized every other passenger on the plane but saw no guys dressed in black. November was the end of the tourist season in Churchill, Manitoba, and these passengers looked like wilderness types coming up for the last tours of the year. Churchill was known as the Polar Bear Capital of the World because the bears traveled through town in the fall to reach ice floes on Hudson Bay. His tour company took clients out to see the polar bears and other wildlife.

He drummed his fingers on his armrest. Then he motioned to the flight attendant.

"Can I have a pop, please?" She nodded and moved away. He tried to lean back, then shifted sideways in his seat, but no matter how he sat, he couldn't avoid seeing the back of Kira's head. She sat ramrod straight. Everything about her screamed *do not approach*.

Kira had made a big show of calling Winnipeg police from the airport. She gave the details and location of the attack and wrote down a police officer's name and number, waving the paper at him as if to say, "See? It's no big deal." And she'd crushed the paper into a ball and shoved it into her leather backpack. None of her behavior made sense to him.

He took the can of pop from the flight attendant and nodded his thanks.

Michael Summers had worked for Webster Technologies' head office in Winnipeg. He'd been planning to fly north to see Kira and had called Lukas to arrange a quick visit.

Lukas let the sweet, cold drink soothe his throat on the way down.

Michael knew Lukas and Kira hadn't spoken in five years. She'd arrived in the spring to work at the Arctic Science Research Centre about twenty kilometers east of town. Lukas had kept his distance after he spotted her grabbing a coffee to go at Ruby's Café on the main drag. Even though his tour groups often crossed paths with the scientists conducting research out on the tundra, he hadn't run into her all season —which was just as well. He figured she'd just run from him again like she had when he proposed.

As the flight settled over the plains heading north, Lukas chewed on the attack on Kira at the cemetery. And the car accident. Michael was— had been—an exemplary driver. They'd raced each other on that highway many times as teenagers. Lukas didn't buy a rollover accident in broad daylight. Were the two events connected? And would she talk to him about the accident, or should he leave her to grieve for a few days?

They flew over the open tundra and banked west. He knew every lake and river below them. The Canadian Shield turned into lush, boreal forest as they headed northeast towards the wild beauty of Hudson Bay. He'd flown to Winnipeg on a whim, jamming a suit into a garment bag for the funeral, after reading about Michael's sudden death. A stupid, freak accident. Unless it wasn't—unless it was tied to Michael's last message, "Hey, I'm flying up Thursday, November 1st. Need to talk to you stat but not over the phone. Kira's not answering, so she's probably out checking her beloved polar bears. See you."

That was all. A cryptic message that could've meant anything. He crushed his pop can in his right hand.

The plane banked left and flew around the town of Churchill, revealing the choppy water and ice of the bay. Lukas loved seeing the expanse of shoreline and rocks every time he was in the air. The wilderness always freed his spirit, as if he'd been holding his breath whenever he'd been away from it. The pilot set the plane down on the asphalt runway and taxied to the terminal.

"Thank you for flying Calm Air today. We look forward to seeing you on your next trip." The flight attendant stood at the front of the plane with a big smile.

Kira stood from her seat and threw her purse over her shoulder. Lukas sighed and grabbed his backpack, motioning another passenger past him. He'd give her some space. A bit of space.

They'd left Winnipeg in sleety rain and freezing temperatures. The sun was still out here and hit him square in his eyes as he went down the few steps of the plane to the tarmac. Although it was -7°C, the late afternoon sun cut across the tundra in watery waves of light, making it seem warmer. Lukas drew in a deep breath. He loved this small, northern subarctic town. Gathered along the shoreline of James Bay, Churchill welcomed travelers going north and south. The people who made it their home were a hardy breed, and he was proud to call it home.

Before he could take another step, Kira planted herself in front of him.

"Are you following me? Or are you going to tell me you live in

7

Churchill?" Her eyes held shadows of fatigue. Now she picked a fight about him being here? He shifted his backpack to give himself time to think.

"Yes, I live here. I've lived here for five years now. I own Guiding Star Enterprises." He could see the instant spark of surprise in her eyes.

"Ah, yes, Daddy's money. I see." She turned away. He couldn't help himself; he put his hand on her arm.

"Not Daddy's money. Mine." She tilted her head towards him but didn't acknowledge his hand on her elbow. "I bought the business from Uncle Henry." He wanted her to understand. He wanted her to *see* what he'd accomplished.

She gave a hollow laugh. "Guess the joke's on me. I've been itching to take one of your whale tours all summer. Now it's too late in the season. Too late for a lot of things."

He dropped his hand and stared hard at her.

"How many of you are there out at the science centre? Do you have a ride?"

"I have a ride, and I'll be fine."

"That place is isolated. You're a good twenty-five minutes out of town." His throat tightened. She'd always been so stubborn. "I want to make sure you're safe."

"Safe from what?" She heaved a sigh, although he could see her 'so what' attitude didn't quite carry to her eyes. "The doors lock from the inside because of the bears. No one's going to get to me in there."

"You don't even know who's trying to get you out here. Men in black don't just abduct people in broad daylight, not even in Winnipeg." He stayed in place, forcing people to move around the two of them. He could be stubborn, too.

Lukas stared at her clear, hazel eyes framed by the wide brows that arched over them. Her skin pinked up in the fresh cold air.

Don't look at her lips. He'd be a goner for sure.

"It happened down there, and now I'm here," Kira said.

She really was stubborn.

"Let it go, Lukas." She turned and headed towards a truck with a young guy in the driver's seat. The sight of her back was just as painful as it was five years ago. Then, she'd jumped up from her restaurant chair and run out the door. She was walking now, but it still punched a hole in his chest.

Let it go, Lukas.

Not very likely.

CHAPTER 2

Kira unlocked the main door to the Arctic Science Research Centre with her swipe card. She braced the door with her hip to prop it open against the brisk wind swirling across the spacious parking lot. The ASRC was a row of interconnected buildings with high-peaked roofs to limit snow buildup. It housed state-of-the-art laboratories and residential accommodations for the dozens of scientists who studied the Arctic eco-system, animals, birds, and climate change.

"Need help carrying those?" Eva Delaney, her undergraduate student, appeared at her side and motioned towards the plastic totes Kira had stacked on top of each other. Eva looked like an anxious, blonde puppy.

"No, this is the last of it." Kira hauled the totes to her bedroom doorway. "But can you grab my key out of my pocket, please?"

Eva pulled a heavy key ring out and jabbed the broad, gold key into the doorknob lock.

"How was your trip?"

She unlatched the door and held it for Kira, who sighed as she settled the plastic boxes on her wide, built-in, wall desk.

"I mean, how was it, considering?"

Eva had the body of a long-distance runner. Her long, straight hair tumbled over her shoulders to frame an exquisite pixie face. She was Kira's shadow and assisted with the polar bear migration research.

"Considering I went down south for a funeral?" Kira shrugged out of her suit jacket and toed off her heeled boots one at a time, flipping them under the desk. "It was," she paused, "extremely stressful."

She sat on her bed and massaged her toes with another sigh of relief. "I had two days to go through Michael's personal belongings and store his furniture. His landlord wanted everything out before November 1st. I'll have to go through those when we're done here for the winter." She jerked her chin towards the three totes on her desk. "These were things I didn't want to store and forget. Personal stuff."

Eva shifted from foot to foot, her lips pressed together.

"What is it?" Kira steeled herself. All she wanted was a hot shower, a huge cup of cocoa, and a pain pill for the headache pounding behind her right eye.

"Professor Birchall." Eva cleared her throat. "He told Ross and me that we've lost the satellite signals on bears X34752 and X34691." She crossed her arms over her chest. "The weather's been unstable, and we thought it would be safer to wait for you. He wasn't happy."

Kira lifted her opposite foot and massaged those toes. She hated wearing heels. "Did he insist you had to go without me?"

"No, but we didn't think it was fair if Professor Birchall didn't want to come with us." She chewed on one of her knuckles. "I don't want to fail this program. I need it to pass my semester."

"You're not going to fail." Kira rose. "I'll take care of it, all right? Besides, we've got those DNA wire traps to examine first in the Wildlife Management Area." She gave her student a half smile. "One thing at a time."

Eva nodded and smiled. "I knew you'd stand by us." She cleared her throat again. "I'll leave you to it then. Good night."

Kira guided her out the door. "Just make sure you're ready to go in the morning, okay? I'm going to grab a shower."

"Sure, no problem." Eva headed down the corridor.

Kira hadn't been exaggerating when she'd told Lukas she'd be safer out here than anywhere else. Every door in the centre had a crash bar that automatically locked because of the polar bears. But thoughts of her near escape in Winnipeg were the last thing on her mind.

The hot water cascading over her neck in the shower eased the knotted muscles of her shoulders and neck. She was brewing a migraine. Whether from the trauma of the attack or the funeral didn't matter. If her headache worsened, she'd be down for a couple of days and useless for going out to check those DNA traps for her research.

Kira's eyes filled with tears. She and Michael hadn't been in touch for two years, and now he was dead. She'd assumed they would reconnect, and she'd have time to explain why she'd fled north and refused to speak to him or anyone. Giving in to her grief, she slid down the shower wall to rest on the floor of the shower stall. Her tears flowed hot and furious.

Where are you, God? Why have you stripped me of everyone I've ever loved? Why am I alone?

As usual, God wasn't answering, although the hot water still soothed her tense neck and shoulder muscles. Another woman entered the shared bathroom and slammed the adjacent stall door. Kira flipped off the water and braced herself to leave her shower and towel off. The foggy mirrors showed she'd gone over the hot water ration. She swiped them with a towel to remove her guilt.

She rubbed lavender essential oil into her temples to relieve the migraine. Then she drew in a deep breath of the calming scent and struggled to put away all thoughts of the attack, Michael, and the funeral.

After putting on a cozy, University-of-Manitoba track suit and thick socks with slippers, Kira headed back to the kitchen to grab an instant cocoa. Sometimes sugar helped with a sick headache. Caffeine always worked. No one was in the kitchen. *Good.* She wouldn't have to field any more questions about Michael's death.

If she could stave off this headache, she'd be able to head out tomorrow and check her DNA wire traps. Kira's project combined sorting DNA samples of fur rubbed off on the barbed wire the bears rubbed against as they ate the seal bait. It allowed them to check the polar bears' current health. And it backed up their satellite data from the bears' collars, which revealed the range each animal traveled during the year.

She'd plastered her room with polar bear posters since she'd first seen them in seventh grade at the Assiniboine Zoo in Winnipeg. Their majestic rolling gait and thick, double-coated fur made them icons of the Canadian North, but climate change was robbing them of their sea ice habitat. Without her project's work of tracking them as they roamed over the tundra to the west and then moved back eastward to venture out onto the ice of Hudson Bay, crucial data on their population and well-being would be lost.

And because they were the highest predator on the food chain, the ecosystem would collapse without them.

She poured boiling water over cocoa in her favorite coffee mug. Michael had given it to her for her high school graduation. The Bible verse "Be Fearless, Joshua 1:7" was printed on it. Back then she'd been fearless with the ignorance of youth. Now she knew the fear that arose from things that happened in the dark. Still, she tried to hold on to the strength in the verse.

The memory of Lukas's strong hands holding her shoulders at the cemetery flitted across her mind as she stirred the cocoa. He'd been her shelter in youth group, during those trying years after their father drove her and Michael to Aunt June's—an aunt by marriage—and abandoned them on her front porch with one suitcase apiece.

Kira closed her eyes, remembering the warmth of Lukas's arm around her shoulder on a sleigh ride while she nestled in beside him. Warm, strong, safe. So, so safe. That's how he'd made her feel.

She couldn't believe she hadn't noticed Lukas around town before now. Churchill was a town of about nine hundred people, although it swelled by several hundreds seasonally with tourists and scientists. Why hadn't he revealed himself to her before now?

Maybe because during their last disastrous date at The Dove restaurant in Winnipeg five years ago, he'd told her during dessert that he loved her and wanted to marry her. She'd taken one look at the diamond solitaire and felt she'd vomit. She'd leapt from her chair, shoved the waiter aside, and run out of the restaurant. No response, no excuse. Just ran away. He'd flown over one thousand kilometers to Winnipeg for the funeral today, and her first impulse was still to flee as far as she could from him. Shaking off the memories making her stomach pitch, she headed back to her room.

An acrid odor hit her as she rounded the main hall corridor. Dark, oily smoke swirled out from under the door to her room. Her mug shattered on the floor as she skidded down the hallway, her slippers tripping her.

Her key remained in the doorknob lock. She paused. She didn't remember leaving her key there, but with the throbbing pain from her oncoming migraine, maybe she'd forgotten it. She cranked the key, burning her fingers, and shoved the door open. She choked and dropped to her knees to see below the inky smoke.

How stupid. Every safety course she'd ever taken said to keep doors shut in case of fire, yet she'd pushed the door open. Smoke poured from the pile of burning fabric atop the comforter on her single bed. Just as she realized it was her clothes burning on the bed, the mixture of oxygen from the hallway and the flames flashed over and threw her backward out of the room.

Kira cracked her head on the doorframe of the opposite room. Dazed, she put her fingers to her left temple and brought them away with a trickle of blood. A searing pain shot through her head as she turned towards her door again.

Something heavy crashed down on her skull. Brilliant flashes of light burst in front of her. Then darkness overpowered her.

Lukas drove his pickup truck hard over the frozen ruts and gullies of the so-called road leading out to the ASRC. Nothing was paved up here, not even the few main streets in town, because of the permafrost. His heavy-duty, 4x4 truck rocked and swayed over the frozen earth. A .308 rifle and a battered shotgun sat in the mounted window rack of his truck cab, although they weren't loaded because Canadian law forbade it. Instead, he carried a box of loud cracker shells as bear deterrent and regular ammo in separate boxes. Up north, everyone needed protection from the polar bears, and he never left his house without them.

He had zero ideas on what he would say to Kira when he saw her again, and no amount of rehearsing at home had helped. She needed to see the Royal Canadian Mounted Police officer in town to make a proper report on that attempted abduction. If he'd phoned her, she'd have cut him off. Better to try to convince her in person.

The faint, whirling, blue and red lights on the horizon came into focus as he approached. He could see people milling outside the ASRC beside the vehicles. The strobing lights of an RCMP truck and the lights of the only volunteer fire truck in town lit up the ASRC walls. But the rotating blades of the crimson air ambulance helicopter caught his attention. He gunned the truck's engine, fishtailing on the packed snow of the parking lot until he pulled in beside the RCMP truck.

He spotted his best friend, RCMP Constable Ben Koper, talking to a young woman and ran over to them.

"What happened?"

Ben raised an eyebrow. "Arson. Eva here's just telling me how she found her boss unconscious in the hallway."

Lukas's heart thudded in his chest. "Wait, is your boss Kira Summers? Where is she? I've got to see her." He swung around in a circle, studying every person in the lot. "Where is she?"

"She's in the air ambulance. They're taking her to the health centre right now," Constable Koper said. "Hey, Lukas!"

Lukas pelted over to the helicopter as the pilot hauled himself up into the cockpit seat. "Wait!" He arrived out of breath. "Wait, I have to go with her."

The pilot adjusted his helmet mic and flipped switches on the roof of the cockpit. "And you are who, buddy? We're in a rush. She needs a CT scan."

"I'm her best friend. Let me ride with her, please."

The man gave him a hard stare and then jerked his head towards the side door. "Long as you don't make it public. Get in."

Lukas yanked open the door, to the surprise of the paramedic inside. He grasped the side handle and hauled himself up, then slid the door shut.

"How is she?" He was almost afraid to look. "Is she... is she burned?"

The pilot lifted off before Lukas could belt himself in. The side swoop of the helicopter made the bottom of his stomach feel like it had dropped between his knees. He grasped the hard edges of the seat to hold himself upright. Engine noise pulsated in his brain.

The pungent scent of scorched hair filled the tight space. Kira lay still, her head bandaged around her temples, a small trickle of blood seeping out of the right side. Blue veins laced her translucent eyelids, and her full lashes were stark black crescents on her pale cheeks. The paramedic was squeezing the resuscitation bag attached to the breathing tube down Kira's throat. The woman stared at him across the gurney.

"Ms. Summers's not stable. She seems to have had a blow to the head. Someone set fire to her room," she shouted. Good thing as he wasn't wearing a helmet, so he couldn't hear the intercoms.

"Her room? With her in it?" Hot anger twisted in his belly. "Who had access to her room?"

"Look, you'll need to ask Constable Koper those questions. We're more worried about her head injury."

The woman handed Lukas the resuscitation bag and indicated he should keep pumping it, while she shone a penlight into Kira's pupils.

"What do you mean 'a hard blow to the head'?" He maintained an even squeezing pressure on the blue bag. "I need to know what happened to her."

"Are you family? Because I've already said too much."

"I'm her... we're practically engaged. Please tell me what you know."

Okay, Lord, technically I'm an ex-boyfriend, but right now, I'm all she's got.

The woman gave a short sigh. "She was groggy when her friend

16

found her. They're going to want to do a CT scan." She leaned over again to read the blood pressure monitor. "I shouldn't have said that, so please keep it to yourself."

"Is her pressure stable?" Pink patches had bloomed on her left cheek and neck. "Do they even have a CT scanner at the health centre?"

"We do. It was donated a month ago by the Milena Scott Foundation. Thank goodness because otherwise we'd have to fly her down to Thompson. If she's got a skull fracture, we need to know asap."

The helicopter banked, and Lukas reached out to catch himself on the edge of Kira's gurney. The pilot swung the helicopter around in a semicircle, and it came to a rest on the squeaky, packed snow outside the health centre in Churchill.

"Get out, please." The woman leaned forward, her kind eyes reminding him of Aunt June's after school when they'd all piled through her front door for snacks. "She's going to be in good hands now."

Lukas nodded. The door swung open, and the pilot gave him a hand down. Then the man grabbed the end of Kira's gurney. He and the paramedic got it on the level parking lot and hurried her inside the sliding doors leading into the ambulance bay.

"Is this the head injury?" A doctor in green scrubs appeared, unshaven and looking as if he'd just awoken, along with another man in scrubs and a nurse.

"Intubated due to possible smoke inhalation; blunt force trauma to the head." The paramedic handed over her Toughbook. "Blood pressure's 110/80; pulse is 64."

The doctor pulled open Kira's eyelids and shone a penlight into her eyes. "Pupils still responsive; let's get her in for a CT right now." He shoved open the heavy doors to the ER and motioned them inside. "And who are you?"

Lukas's lungs squeezed as if he'd run ten kilometers. "Her boyfriend. Her friend. Please, she has no family. I need to make sure she's okay." His speech rattled off like automatic gunfire. The doctor put a hand on his shoulder and squeezed.

"Wait here. I'll come for you when I know something." He peered at Lukas. "Okay? Got it?"

Lukas nodded. Kira's gurney disappeared down the hall.

He rested his back against the wall and rubbed his eyes.

Lord, You're all she's got... Please, please, don't let that be a skull fracture. Lord, take care of her and heal her. I'm putting her in Your hands. Amen.

Blood rushed in his ears. He put his head back and knocked it against the concrete wall a few times. *This is so unfair! First Michael, now Kira? I didn't even get to the funeral, and now she's torn away...*

He forced air in through his nose, held it, then breathed it out through his mouth a few times. *Torn away, like Abby...*was the thought he hadn't wanted to finish. He closed his eyes and made himself take more deep breaths. He and Kira were in the past, but he could still do right by her. For Michael's sake.

Get your act together, Tanner. Guard your heart, but do what needs to be done.

Lukas pushed off the wall and went in search of the chapel.

CHAPTER 3

Lukas put his vending machine coffee on the oak table in the waiting lounge. A young woman sat in the corner of the room, knitting in silence. He blew out a sigh as he sat back on the leather couch.

Lukas thumbed open his phone and pressed video call. The hot coffee warmed his stomach while he sat through three rings. Ruby Gallagher appeared on his phone screen, out of breath and balancing a child on her hip.

"Hello, Lukas. We just finished our bath, didn't we, honey?"

Lukas smiled at the little girl bundled in a towel. She tilted her head side to side and giggled.

"Hey, Sophie! How's my beautiful daughter?"

His little girl reached for the phone and tried to kiss it, wriggling forward so fast she almost fell out of the woman's arms.

"Now, Sophie, hang on." The woman disappeared. Then his sweet girl's face filled the screen. "Here's your father," she said.

"Hey, Sophie, Daddy loves you." Lukas blew her a kiss. "Daddy's going to be late tonight." His daughter put a finger in her mouth and turned her head to the side. "Ruby, I hate to ask..."

"It's fine, Lukas. I can stay till you get home. My granddaughter's closing up the café for me."

"Well, I'm at the health centre," he said.

"What happened?" Ruby's face came into full view on the phone. "You okay?"

"It's a close friend of mine; someone attacked her, and I'm waiting for news." He sighed. "It could be awhile."

Sophie grabbed at the phone.

"No problem, Lukas. I can stay as late as you need. All night if I have to." She jiggled Sophie on her hip. "Miss Bright Eyes and I will be just fine, right, honey?" Her face filled the phone screen. "Don't worry, Lukas. See you whenever."

He smiled into the phone. "You're a lifesaver, Ruby. Give Daddy a kiss, my love." He blew another kiss at the screen. Sophie's lips filled the screen, and she giggled.

"Bye-bye, sweetheart." He touched her face on the screen and then flicked the phone off. He leaned back on the couch and closed his eyes. Sophie had only been an infant when his wife, Abby, died. A freak snowmobile accident on New Year's Day two-and-a-half years ago had left Abby in a coma, and she'd never woken. He knew all about Kira's pain at the cemetery. He knew the piercing ache when reality hit that the person you loved was never coming back.

Ben appeared in the lounge doorway. Taking his gloves off and settling his tall, lean frame into a chair, he asked, "Any news?"

Lukas shook his head. "She's having a CT scan. The paramedic told me she'd been hit in the head with a heavy object. What did you find at the scene?"

Ben removed his muskrat hat and unzipped his parka. "No weapon or object with blood on it. The fire's out. The room is pretty much destroyed because of water damage. Eva said there's some plastic totes missing. I guess Kira brought four back with her. This one was under the desk, closest to the door, so I brought it with me." He gestured to the plastic tote he'd put on the floor. "And Kira's laptop is gone."

He flipped open his notebook. "Eva was getting ready for bed and said she hadn't seen Kira for about an hour. The fire alarm sounded, and she found Kira lying semi-conscious in the hallway when she went to evacuate."

"Those totes were her brother Michael's personal effects. Who would want them?" Lukas tapped his fingers on the table. "His funeral was today in Winnipeg."

"I'm sorry to hear that. I'm surprised she didn't take some time off. Were they close?"

Lukas shrugged. "Not for a while. He phoned me last week and said he was coming up here Thursday the first. Said he hadn't gotten in touch with Kira, figured she was out working, but..."

"But what?" Ben leaned forward in his chair.

"He needed to talk about something. Something important he couldn't say over the phone. Then he died in a rollover accident last Saturday, October 27th, on clean pavement during daylight." Lukas straightened. "Kira's still processing his death, but I question the circumstances of the accident. Any chance you can get the accident report from the police down in Winnipeg?"

Ben tapped his chin with his pen. "No reason to legally. What makes you believe it was more than an accident?"

Lukas steepled his fingers. "She was attacked today at the cemetery. I wanted her to file a report in Winnipeg, and she called it in, but it's not going to get the police searching for the guys. I was on my way out to ASRC to convince her to talk to you about it."

"Attacked? The same day someone attacks her here?" Ben snapped his notebook shut. "Any cop will tell you there are no coincidences in police work."

Lukas stood and paced the length of the small lounge. "I know! She's so stubborn, she's just..." He stopped short and stared at the wall while resting his fists on his hips. "I don't even know who she is anymore."

Ben cleared his throat behind his hand. "You've known her how long?"

Lukas turned back to him. "We dated in high school and university. I knew her brother, Michael, first; we were best friends throughout high school. I met her at our church youth group. She was a wild child, but Michael dragged her there every Wednesday." His expression softened. "Once upon a time, I knew Kira very well." He drew in a breath.

"I see." Ben shifted in his chair. Cleared his throat again. "Did she tell you about this attack in Winnipeg?"

"I was right there when it happened. A guy jumped out of a van and tried to haul her into it. She fought him off, and when she fell, I grabbed him. The driver flashed something. It might've been a gun, I don't know. Then they took off."

Ben jotted notes. "What kind of van? And can you describe them?"

"White van. I didn't get the make—or a license plate." Lukas flexed his hands in frustration. "I grabbed her as they were racing out of there. One wore a ski mask, and the driver had on sunglasses."

"She didn't think this was worth reporting?" Ben raised an eyebrow.

"No, and I don't know why. Maybe she was too traumatized." He sat down. "Or, maybe it's to do with Michael, but she won't talk about him or anything else."

The doctor appeared in the doorway. Nodding at Ben, he said, "She's been in and out of consciousness. The CT scan shows she's got a concussion. She was fortunate there was no actual skull fracture." He rubbed the scruff on his jaw. "But she sustained a good blow to the head. She's got ten stitches on the right side of her scalp, but whatever she was hit with didn't break the skull."

"What's the prognosis?" Lukas held his breath.

"She has to take time off. No computer work, reading, texting, nothing with a screen. Her brain needs to heal itself. No idea how long it'll take."

Ben stood up. "Two attacks in a twenty-four-hour period mean I can contact the Winnipeg police. Let me know when she can have visitors. I'll need to get a statement." He picked up the semi-melted plastic tote and handed it to Lukas. "This is all that's left of her brother's things, Eva told me. I'm sure Kira will want to see them."

"Thanks," Lukas said. "I'll make sure she gets it."

The doctor turned to him. "Do you want to see her? She needs to rest, but it might help if she knows someone is here."

Lukas picked up his parka and lifted the tote to carry it with both arms. "Yeah, I need to see her."

"She's in Room 12," said the doctor.

Stopping outside her room, Lukas prepared himself. Soft light fell on Kira's face from the overhead lamp. She had an oxygen tube in her nose, and an IV fluid bag hung at her side.

A nurse finished taking her blood pressure and jotted it down in the notebook she carried in her pocket. She turned to Lukas. "The IV's giving her antibiotics for the burns and will keep her hydrated. Don't stay too long."

Lukas nodded. He came alongside her bed and pulled over the one chair in the tiny room. Her eyelids fluttered open.

"Hey..."

Her hands were still bandaged. He gently pushed her bangs back on her forehead. "It's me. How're you feeling?"

She sighed and struggled to focus on his face. "Head hurts." She tried to stretch but stopped herself. "Water?" she croaked.

"Sure." He grabbed the plastic cup on her bedside table and held the straw to her lips. "Slowly, now."

Kira sipped and grimaced. "Throat hurts, too."

"Take it easy." He put the cup back. "I'm not leaving you. Rest now, okay?"

She nodded and closed her eyes. Her right hand came up and rested on his forearm.

"Sorry..." she whispered.

"Shh." He pulled the plastic chair over to the bed. "I'm not going anywhere."

Her breathing quieted as she fell asleep. Lukas turned the lamp down and tried to get comfortable in the chair. No one was getting past him. No one.

Perforated ceiling tiles were all she could see. Her heart pumped with a fear she couldn't name. Her head felt like it would explode from piercing pain. Her throat burned. She raised her hands to check them and winced at the bandages. She glanced to the right. A navy-blue parka lay over the back of the chair. She couldn't remember what had happened or to whom the parka belonged.

She felt the smooth bandages that circled her head like a tissue paper crown. Tears dribbled down her cheeks. Why, she didn't know. Something bad had happened. She wasn't sure where she was... but her head! The pain crushed her head like a vise.

Lukas entered with a steaming cup of coffee in his hand. Dizziness overcame her, and she felt her insides roll and shift.

"Whoa." He grabbed the kidney-shaped basin off the table and held her hair as she vomited. "Easy now; you're okay." He patted her face with a cool cloth. "You've got a concussion, so this is just part of it."

She moaned and closed her eyes. Wonderful! How enchanting to throw up in front of the one man she'd insulted beyond belief. Her throat burned all the way down as she swallowed.

"Here, take a tiny sip." He offered her water through a straw. "Do you know where you are?"

She moved her head to say no, but pain splintered behind her eyes again.

"You're in the health centre. Someone cracked you on the head." Lukas quickly rinsed out the kidney basin and put it back within her reach. "You've got mild burns on your hands and ten stitches on the side of your head." He leaned on the side rail of her bed, his eyes intent on her face. "Do you remember anything?"

"No," she rasped. "Why's my throat so sore?"

"Smoke," he said. "Someone set a fire in your room. Eva found you."

"My room?" It hurt to think. "I don't remember anything. What time is it?"

Lukas checked his watch. "Nearly seven a.m. Just rest till they bring you breakfast." He gently touched her arm. "I'll be right here."

"Okay." She closed her eyes.

"Rest," he said as he tucked the blanket around her shoulders. He brushed a few errant curls behind her ear and let his his touch linger on the bandage swathing her head.

She heard the door to her room bang against the wall and forced her eyes open, trying to focus on the figure at the end of her bed.

"Am I interrupting?" She heard a woman's cool, elegant voice.

"She's not receiving visitors at the moment," Lukas said. "You can leave those with me."

Leave what? Kira tried to move her head to the left. *Ow.*

A huge bouquet of pink carnations appeared at her bedside. A monstrous bouquet. The scent made her stomach squirm again. The woman behind the bouquet put them perilously close to the edge of her bedside table.

She didn't recognize the woman who appeared to be in her mid-forties: a bleached blonde with straight hair curled under at her chin. Her face was covered with blotchy freckles, and a thin nose ended in a dimple that detracted from the symmetry of her face. Model-thin, the woman peeled off aboriginal, beaded, leather gloves to reveal crayon-red nails. Her lipstick matched. Without asking anyone's permission, the woman shrugged off her parka and sat in the chair Lukas had vacated.

She leaned forward and touched Kira's hand on the covers. "My dear, dear Kira. I'm Alison Webster. Your brother, Michael, worked for me." Her grey eyes were edged in startling black, spiky mascara. "I'm so sorry I couldn't make it to his funeral. I hope you'll accept these flowers from the company as a tribute to Michael."

Alison Webster? The owner of Webster Technologies? What was she doing in Churchill? *What a creepy thing to do—bring funeral flowers to a live person in the hospital.* Thinking made her woozy.

Lukas leaned over Kira's bed into the woman's space. "She needs her rest. I'm not going to say it again. Do I need to get the nurse in here?"

Alison motioned him away as though swiping at a mosquito. "I'm merely here to give her my condolences." She patted Kira's hand again. "If there's anything you need, dear, anything at all, you call my secretary." She fished a business card out of her leather purse and parked it in the bouquet. "Do you know what Michael was working on before he died?"

Kira tried not to turn her head too far lest the room spin again. She rasped, "No, we hadn't spoken in a while." She stared at Lukas, begging him with her gaze to get rid of the stranger and the pungent flowers.

"That's it, I'm getting the nurse," Lukas said.

"Really?" Alison raised her over-plucked eyebrows. "I thought you two were close."

Kira shook her head a tiny bit. Even that pained her. "I have no idea what he was working on. Don't you know? You're his boss, aren't you?"

Alison's laugh sounded fake, even to Kira. "Not his direct boss, dear. Anyway," she leaned forward in the chair, "I was just making conversation."

"Well, make it somewhere else." Lukas was back in the doorway with a nurse peeking over his shoulder. "You need to clear out."

"Ms. Summers is seeing only family. You can visit tomorrow," the petite nurse said.

Alison picked up her expensive, wool parka and nodded again. "Take care, dear. We'll be in touch. I'll make sure human resources calls you to deal with Michael's paperwork." She moved to the doorway with the smell of her heavy perfume following her. "Michael was one of our up-and-comers. He'll be missed." She turned to Lukas. "Will you let me know when she's up and around?"

Lukas eased the woman out the door. "She can call you when she feels up to it."

The nurse checked Kira's blood pressure and the level of IV fluid left in the hanging bag. Kira lost track of time until loud male voices brought her to with a start. Angry voices—were they talking about her?

Lukas stepped up to her bedside as the police officer strode into the room.

"I'm not leaving her here alone and unprotected. I can take her home and keep her safe," Lukas said.

"I've called in reinforcements. Another officer will be here in a day or two." The constable nodded to her. "We're down an officer. But we can keep you safe, Kira. I'm Constable Ben Koper."

"Either she gets twenty-four-hour protection here or she's coming home with me." Lukas stood in a familiar stance, legs planted with his fists on his hips. He used to stand the same way on the debate team and lost points for his posture. Her dry lips cracked when she tried to smile at the officer.

"What did the doctor say?" Ben asked. "Can she even be moved?"

"I have written instructions on caring for her burns, and Dr. Stedman gave me concussion protocol. She has a follow-up appointment in seven days."

Ben turned back to her, causing his parka to brush against the end of her bed.

"If you want to stay in hospital, I can have one of the Canadian Rangers outside your door till the fill-in police officer arrives from Lynn Lake."

"They're not armed," Lukas interrupted. "They're trained in search and rescue, not security. Someone tried to kill her!"

The amount of emotion between the two men overwhelmed her.

Someone tried to kill me? She still couldn't pull up the memories.

"Can't I go back to ASRC?" Her voice still rasped. "If the doctor says I can, I want to go back there."

Ben squeezed his muskrat hat between both hands and blew out his breath. "It's still a crime scene till the forensics identification services tech from Thompson arrives tomorrow."

Crime scene? She closed her eyes. She would *not* cry in front of these men.

Lukas put his hands on her bed rail. "Kira, you need someone with you for the next twenty-four hours—the doc said preferably forty-eight. Around the clock. The hotels are packed because it's polar bear season. I can keep you safe and watch over you at my place."

"And when can I go back to work?"

"Not till after your follow-up appointment. So, you can stay for a week or whenever they release your room to you. It's no problem; I've got plenty of room."

He had the earnest look of her old border collie, Jasper. And Jasper always got what he wanted from her.

"I've got tracking work to do..." She tried to sit up, but Lukas gently put his hands on her shoulders.

"No work till next week. Your brain's concussed, and it needs to rest. Maybe for longer than a week. No working on the computer, no reading, no texting, no TV." He squeezed her right shoulder. "Doctor's orders, not mine. I don't even have a TV."

Lukas without a TV? That made her smile. In university, Lukas had every tech toy going, along with a huge television screen for gaming with his pals.

Constable Koper put on his hat, pulled down the ear flaps, and zipped his parka. "Fine. If I get a chance, I'll drive by your place to check on both of you. I'll call you when the new officer arrives. Meantime," he turned to Kira, "take care of yourself, Ms. Summers. And do what the doctor says; it's essential to your recovery."

Kira closed her eyes and slowly opened them again. Even that hurt. "I don't think I'll have much choice in the matter."

Lukas clasped the hand Ben offered. "We'll be fine. Keep me posted on what you find out down south."

"Down south?" Kira asked.

"I'll keep you both posted." He gave her a two-finger salute. "Get better, Ms. Summers." Then he disappeared out the door.

"After you eat, we can head out. Unless you want to rest longer—it's up to you."

"I don't want to keep you from your own work."

Lukas leaned down and caressed the top of her head. His breath fell soft on her face, and he was close enough she could see the dark ring of blue around his irises. "Right now, you're my only concern. My next tour isn't arriving till Wednesday—two whole days from now." He withdrew and stood. She felt a tinge of pain at the loss of his closeness.

"The nurse is bringing you some breakfast. I'll be just down the hall."

For a second, she thought he would kiss her forehead when he bent over her again. He hesitated, his lips a breath away from her skin, and when he pulled away, she felt the room lose its warmth. He ducked his head and headed out the door.

The cheery nurse brought her breakfast tray, but Kira had no appetite. Watery porridge. Toast with butter, no jam, two orange slices, and a cup of lukewarm coffee. Yay. She leaned back on her pillow. *Oh Lukas, please have a huge, huge coffeemaker!* It didn't matter if she still had the migraine because her entire head was now concussed and in pain anyway.

She knew Lukas went into "control" mode whenever he was anxious, and it seemed nothing had changed in that regard. He'd even bossed around the sole police officer in town. She thought she'd overhead them laughing like friends earlier, so she couldn't be sure. But she suspected it was only by the grace of God she was alive. And while that had nothing to do with Lukas, she knew better than to try to stop him when he got his mind set on something. Guess she was under his protection—at least for now.

CHAPTER 4

Lukas's pickup truck rattled her bones and made her vision swim as they drove out of town. Kira hoped her meager breakfast would stay down so she wouldn't embarrass herself again by tossing it. Kira gritted her teeth and closed her eyes against the up and down motion of the truck. She shrugged her shoulders deeper into the ratty parka the nurse had given her from the lost-and-found, along with a pair of over-sized mukluks. The thin cotton scrubs she wore underneath weren't doing a great job of keeping the cold air out.

"How much farther?" Her voice sounded tinny even to herself.

"Almost there. Tell me if you need me to stop."

"I'm good," she said. Okay, maybe not, but she was trying.

She must be crazy, or her head injury was worse than she thought. Spending a couple of days with him in his home after rejecting his marriage proposal five years ago? What could she say? *Hey, I ran out of the restaurant because I couldn't believe you'd still love me if you knew the truth? That someone ravaged and discarded me like trash? That I knew being damaged goods wouldn't live up to your expectations of perfection?*

She closed her eyes again. She'd thought she'd run far enough from Lukas and anyone who might have guessed the truth. Now here she was

depending on him to take care of her for at least a week. Being depen-
dent rankled her, and she bit her bottom lip to hold back tears.

He'd been a gentleman ever since Michael's funeral. He hadn't
brought up the past. All right, he was his usual overprotective self. And
she hadn't been honest about her feelings, but she was terrified to be
alone since the fire.

"Is Eva okay?"

"She's fine," Lukas said. "She wasn't in your room. Good thing you
weren't either, or it might've been a different ending."

Kira nodded but couldn't think of anything else to say. No way was
she letting on how petrified she felt. She'd gone this long without
confiding in him about the absolute worst horror of her life. She could
keep her feelings to herself. She closed her eyes as memories washed
over her.

*In high school, Michael had taken on the role of the father who'd
abandoned both of them He'd dragged her to his church youth group even
though at first she'd wanted nothing to do with it. But Lukas Tanner was
the shining star who drew everyone into his orbit. He drove a '67 blue
convertible Mustang. He'd grown up in the church. His father was
chairman of the deacon's board, and they wintered in Florida every year.
And he wanted to date her, Kira Summers, whose Aunt June bought her
church dresses from Value Village. Lukas didn't care. So she didn't care.*

*Lukas could quote scripture to her all night long. He had all the
answers or thought he did. He lived in the moment, and nothing was too
dangerous not to be fun. She did her best to keep up and follow in his
wake. She had once loved him with her whole heart.*

She opened her eyes and glanced sideways at him in the truck. This
version of Lukas was dressed down, driving an ancient truck, not a
perfect, blue, '67 Mustang. His brows were drawn together, and his jaw
clenched as he turned into another road. They bounced along frozen
ruts leading up to a property with an aluminum-sided modular home
near the road. He'd referred to it as a "cabin", but it stood as square and
modern as any other house in Churchill. She could see a small, wooden
barn at the back of the yard with a chain link enclosure beside it. Eight

cubed, wooden structures inside it housed the dogs that ran beside the fence, leaping and barking at the truck.

"My sled team," he said, gesturing towards the dogs. "We've won a few races up here. Sometimes, my guests like taking a sled ride as part of their tour package." He glanced over at her again. "You like dogs, I seem to remember."

"Love them," she enthused. "It's hard to think of an animal I don't like."

Ugh! Don't try so hard. You don't need to impress him or anyone else.

The dogs continued barking as the truck pulled into the yard. A large, mixed-breed dog raced up to the truck and jumped at her window, scrabbling at the glass.

"Whoa!" She jumped in her seat. "He scared me."

"That's Gunner. He won't hurt you." Lukas leaned out his window. "Gunner, down, boy!"

Lukas wheeled the truck up to the front deck. Then he turned to reach behind the seat. "I bought you some clothes. I guessed on your sizes, but I think they're close." His mouth quirked up in that adorable way she remembered so well.

She opened her mouth to speak, but he held up his hand.

"You can pay me back later. Let's get you inside and warmed up."

She nodded and slid down from the cab. Gunner ran circles in the snow around Lukas's legs. Lukas held the bag of clothes up out of the way and threw snow at the dog trying to catch the flakes in its mouth.

The front door opened, and a middle-aged woman stepped out. Kira's stomach churned. He hadn't said anything about his living arrangements or any romantic ties. And she hadn't asked. She hesitated at the bottom of the steps. It was none of her business even if the woman in front of her had been closer to her age. She and Lukas were in the past.

"Come in, you two. You're going to freeze." The woman motioned them indoors. The steps were shoveled, and smells teased them from inside the house. Stew? Soup? Something hot and delicious made her realize her porridge had done little to fill her.

"You must be Kira." The woman gave her a brief hug. "I'm Ruby. Just come on in and I'll get you a hot drink. Tea? Coffee?"

Kira patted Ruby's back awkwardly with her bandaged hands.

"A hot chocolate would be great," Kira said, "if you have any?"

Lukas stepped around Kira after kicking the snow off his boots. He put down her plastic tote and a bag of clothes in the front hallway. "Hot chocolate is one of the four food groups in this house. Let's all have some please, Ruby."

Ruby bustled towards the open-concept kitchen to the left. "Putting the kettle on right now."

"Da-Dee! Da-Dee!" a high, feminine voice pealed. Kira took in a rush of pink clothes and bunny slippers as a small child launched herself at Lukas.

Daddy? She really should've asked more questions before she agreed to this scheme.

Where there was a child, there was usually a wife. Kira's heart thudded against her chest.

His wife. Lord, I'm not prepared for this, I can't do this...

Lukas swung his daughter around in a circle and buried his mouth against her neck, making bubble noises that set her off in another peal of laughter. He pretended to be devouring her, to her delight.

"Da-Dee! You home!"

Lukas smacked one last kiss on her cheek. "I'm home, sweet pea, and here's a lady for you to say 'hi' to." He swung around to face Kira, while resting his daughter on his hip. The child pulled her stuffed bunny up to her face and peeked around the ears. Kira started to say "hello" but stopped. The child's long, dark blonde hair curled around her shoulders. Her rosy cheeks shone with good health, and her smile was radiant. She wore hot pink, wire-rimmed glasses. Her eyes were slanted and almond-shaped. Dark blue with silver glints in them.

Lukas hitched her up higher on his hip and cleared his throat.

"This is my daughter, Sophie. Sophie, can you say hello to Kira?"

Sophie buried her face in Lukas's shoulder and held on for dear life.

"She's always a bit shy with strangers." He paused. "Sophie has

Down Syndrome. She's three years old now, aren't you, lovey?"

Sophie held up four fingers.

"No, just three, honey." Lukas folded down one of her fingers, and she giggled again. She held up three fingers, then stuck her thumb in her mouth.

Kira's cheeks flamed hot. Her feet might as well have been rooted to the floor. She gave herself a shake.

"Hey, Sophie!" Kira forced a step forward and waved a "hello" motion with her right hand. "How're you? Glad Daddy's home, I'll bet."

Sophie wiggled down and ran towards Ruby, who was pouring boiling water into mugs.

Why had she hesitated? Lukas hadn't shared anything with her, but she was a scientist. She knew about one in 800 babies were born with Down Syndrome. She wanted to apologize for her reaction, but the moment was gone. Lukas motioned for her to go ahead of him.

"Let's get that hot chocolate, all right?" Judging by the tic in his jaw, he'd caught her hesitation.

Nice going. Now he thinks you're shocked his daughter has a disability. What's the matter with you?

She followed him to the table. *Stop thinking about how terrified you are, and show him some appreciation for how far he's gone out of his way to help you in the past thirty-six hours.* Kira took the proffered hot chocolate from Ruby. Maybe later she'd find a moment to ask Ruby where his wife was, but whatever the story was here, it was none of her business.

Lukas woke the next morning with a stiff neck and shoulder. Kira had taken the master bedroom, and he'd slept on the couch. His dogs were an early warning alarm system; still, it was better sleeping outside her door. The house was a sprawling, open-concept bungalow with two bedrooms and a den across the back. He'd bought it from Uncle Henry before he and Abby were married. Their four acres held flat tundra with stunted trees filling in the eastern edge of the property. The famous Northern

Lights always showed up in their "piece of heaven," as Abby used to call it.

Abby. In his haste to bring Kira here, he hadn't given one thought to the need to introduce Sophie to her or mention his marriage. Well, at least now she knew he hadn't pined away for the past five years. Not that Abby had been a consolation prize. Lukas winced as he straightened, his neck pinched from sleeping crooked on the couch.

He rolled up his sheets and blanket. He'd driven himself crazy trying to forget Kira's rejection. Back then, everything had come easily to him, and he'd figured her running out of the restaurant was just her way of playing hard to get. But after twenty-one text messages, Michael had stepped in and told him to back off. Kira had refused to see him or speak to him. And that was that—the end.

It wasn't just his pride destroyed. He'd loved Kira with all the innocence of first love. So when Uncle Henry had emailed about his terminal cancer, Lukas had flown up north on impulse. All his life, he'd been closer to Uncle Henry than his own father, so helping him keep the business running was a no-brainer. And the wide-open Arctic spaces had split open and healed the anger simmering in his heart.

He'd met Abby when he'd approached the town council about ways Guiding Star Enterprises could attract more tourists. Her warm, brown eyes and quick smile had thawed his heart, and they were engaged by spring.

His father had refused to attend the wedding. His dad had already cut him off when he rejected the executive position in his dad's company in favour of staying in Churchill. Literally. With a letter from his dad's lawyer, informing Lukas he was removed from his father's will.

Remembering, Lukas poured fresh water into the coffeemaker as he tried to wake up. He'd sent his dad a couple of wedding photos and then a picture of Sophie when she was one month old. There'd been nothing but deafening silence from his father. He figured the relationship, if there ever was one in the future, was in God's hands.

The coffee burbled. Lukas checked for eggs, bacon, and fruit. Sophie loved bananas. She'd be up soon, and his day would start. Closing the fridge, he headed for the shower in the master bedroom. Kira's door was closed. Good, maybe he could get Sophie fed before Kira woke.

He tried not to remember the shocked look on Kira's face last night. No, a mixture of shock and surprise. What did he expect? He'd sprung everything on her. He owed it to Michael to keep Kira safe and get to the bottom of these attacks. *And that's all you're going to do, keep her safe,* he told himself as he tossed his T-shirt in the laundry basket. *Not help her fall in love with your adorable daughter.*

Kira lay perfectly still in the guest bed. Sleep had been a blessing, but now her head pain came back full force. If she moved, either her head hurt or her hands did. She lay and listened to the sounds of Lukas moving around his home, then to the sound of the shower.

No shower for her today. She couldn't bear the thought of water pinging on her scalp. She brought her hands up in front of her face. Yep, still wrapped up in gauze. Ruby had offered to come back to redo them for her, but Lukas had said he could do whatever Kira needed.

Before Ruby had left, Kira'd tried to ask where Lukas's wife was, but Ruby had whispered it wasn't her story to tell. Ruby'd given her hand a squeeze and then kissed Sophie goodbye on the way out the door. They'd all waved from the front window as Ruby drove away in her truck to head home.

Staring at the ceiling, Kira took stock of her past two days. She had no idea who'd want to kidnap her or why. She wasn't wealthy, nor was her brother. She shared only wildlife photos or travel shots on her social media accounts and kept her private life private. One of thirty Canadian and international research scientists at the ASRC, she dealt with government contracts but nothing so secret it warranted violence.

She pulled herself up in the bed. Another major effort got her legs over the side, and she pressed her fingers to her temples. Lukas had offered her a pain pill in the middle of the night. Though she needed one now, she didn't want to be foggy all day. She wanted to help Lukas with his dogs or whatever he needed around the house, not be a burden to him.

He'd bought her a sweat suit and some T-shirts, along with some runners, socks and underwear. The T-shirt had long sleeves, so she eased them over her bandaged hands. She zipped up the sweat suit's hoodie. Checking her face in the mirror, she applied aloe vera to her cheeks, lips, and neck. The surface burns looked better already, although maybe that was wishful thinking.

Kira opened the dresser drawer, looking for a comb or brush. A sapphire-blue, velvet jewelry box lay in the back right corner of the drawer. Glancing at the closed bedroom door, she quietly removed the box and opened it. Two gold wedding rings studded with pavé diamonds rested on the satin interior. A dried red rose and a bookmark lay beside a delicate, gold-filigreed cross with tiny sparkling diamonds in its center. Kira ran her fingertip over the cross and then lifted it out of the long narrow box. She held it up to the light.

His wife's cross. It had to be. So, he'd married a Christian, which meant he still had his faith. The diamonds twinkled in the sunlight. The bookmark read:

"A wife of noble character who can find? She is worth far more than rubies." Proverbs 31:1.

Diamonds symbolized an everlasting love. Rubies were for wives of noble character. Her traitorous eyes filled with tears again. She laid the fragile necklace back in the box and closed it with a snap.

Bitter anger closed her throat.

My jewelry should be in here, God. My ring should be on Lukas's finger. Why did You let that happen to me? What did I ever do to deserve it?

She slammed the drawer shut with more force than she intended, then stood silent and listened to see if Lukas would come to the door.

But he wasn't wearing his wedding ring. It was in the jewelry box. Her mind whirled with possibilities as she patted at her tears with the backs of her bandaged hands. She could handle this—she *would* handle it. Should she ask where his wife was or wait for him to tell her? Putting

37

her hand on the doorknob, she inhaled a deep cleansing breath and shot up an arrow prayer for wisdom, then walked out to the great room.

Lukas stood with his back to the room as he moved between two frying pans and the toaster in the kitchen area at the far end of the house. His broad shoulders filled out a frayed Winnipeg Jets hockey jersey, and his hair, still damp from his shower, clustered in wavy curls on his head. Her throat tightened. Here he was, larger than life and still handsome enough to take her breath away.

Kira tamped down those thoughts. In her wildest—okay, maybe not her *wildest* dreams–she'd never imagined Lukas being divorced. But why else would he have his wife's wedding ring in his drawer? And custody of his daughter? Had his rebellious streak gotten him caught up with someone who'd broken his heart a second time?

Sophie colored at the kitchen table, swinging her feet under her chair. Soft, classical music played on the radio. Kira cast a quick glance around the living area, checking for photos of Lukas and his wife. There were none, just a studio portrait of Sophie. Last night, she'd been so out of it she hadn't noticed the sleek Danish modern furniture warmed up with touches of red in the couch pillows and area rug. Cozy. And not decidedly feminine or masculine. His wife's decorating?

She cleared her throat. "Good morning." She walked over to the table. "How'd you sleep?"

Lukas flipped a couple of eggs over in the pan. "Hey, how are you? We slept great, didn't we, darling?" He bent over to nuzzle Sophie, who giggled and rubbed his nose with hers.

"Are you hungry?" His eyes crinkled at the edges. Outdoor living agreed with him. In spite of it being winter, he'd kept some of his summer tan. "I made bacon and eggs, but I have hot cereal if you'd rather."

Kira sat down opposite Sophie. "I am a bit hungry. Do you have coffee?"

"Coming right up." He poured two mugs. "Sugar? Creamer? Fake creamer?"

She smiled at Sophie but answered him. "Fake creamer is fine, and bacon and eggs would be heaven. Thank you."

She blew out a sigh as he handed her the doctored coffee. "I need one of those pain pills, but they're not in my... room." She forced herself to look straight at him. "Do you have them?"

He wiped his hands on his jeans. "Sorry, I put them up on the fridge to make sure Sophie didn't take them off your bedside table." He reached up and grabbed the small bottle.

"Oh, I'm sorry, I didn't think..." Her cheeks flushed red. Of course, a toddler would be in danger near a bottle of pain pills.

"No problem." He handed her the bottle and a glass of water. "You can have two if you need or want them. Dr. Stedman told me it's important to keep it up in your system so the pain doesn't become debilitating."

She shook out a white pill. "I think I can manage with one." She swallowed it with a gulp of water and took a deep breath.

Lukas set full plates before both her and Sophie, then seated himself at the head of the table. "Shall we say the blessing?"

Sophie put her tiny hand in his. She regarded Kira steadily across the table, her eyes the color of crushed cornflowers. Her other hand went under the table. Lukas gave his hand to Kira and said nothing. Kira took his hand and bowed her head. She hadn't prayed over her food since God had abandoned her in her dorm room six years ago.

"Heavenly Father, thank you for this beautiful day and this food You have provided. Amen," Lukas said.

"Ahhh-men!" said Sophie.

Gunner appeared at Kira's side, butting his head in her lap. She petted his silky ears, and he sat beside her chair. His bottom wiggled, and his tail thumped on the floor. Kira gave him another couple of strokes on the top of his head before he flopped at her feet, letting out a deep sigh.

Lukas helped Sophie cut up her eggs and bacon. She got up on her knees in the chair to reach for her glass of milk. They shared a language shorthand. Lukas knew what Sophie was saying even if it was only one or two words at a time. Sophie giggled when he told her not to put two pieces of bacon in her mouth. She pursed her lips to make them move up and down like pincers until he laughed out loud and planted a kiss on her forehead.

Kira swallowed her coffee even though her appetite was gone. This cozy breakfast could've been her life with Lukas. She blinked back tears.

"So," he turned his attention to Kira, "how's your head?"

"Still pounding. I can't believe Dr. Stedman said I can't use the computer, though. I'm going to be so behind on my tracking."

"No computer, texting, TV, or screen time of any kind." Lukas pushed back his empty plate. "I want you to follow the concussion protocol. Dr. Stedman knows what he's talking about."

Kira grimaced. "What am I supposed to do? I can't sleep all the time."

Lukas stood up and brought the coffeepot back over to the table. "How are you, really?"

This morning, his ice-blue eyes held flecks of deep blue. And she had forgotten how that killer smile could send warmth flooding throughout her body. She stared into her coffee as he poured the creamer into it.

"What you could expect," she said. She held the steaming cup of coffee in both hands carefully because of the bandages. "It's not like anyone's tried to kill me recently." She raised her eyes to his. "Sorry, I've really tried to give up the sarcasm."

"You have every right to be mad, or scared, but the Kira I used to know will get through this." He touched her right hand in a light caress and then withdrew it.

She closed her eyes for a second, wishing he'd hold her hand forever and tell her everything would be all right.

"I'm sorry I was so... angry at the cemetery." She played with the handle of her table knife. "I never got to say goodbye, you know?" Tears welled up in her eyes. "We were both always so busy, and I thought we had time."

"Michael loved you, Kira. Never doubt that," Lukas said. "You drove him crazy in high school, but he was so proud of you." He laughed, and the sound warmed her. "Michael was proud of all your career accomplishments, too."

Lukas wiped Sophie's mouth with a wet cloth and helped her down from her chair. "Scoot! Go play now. The big people are talking."

"I'm sorry; I seem to be blubbering all the time." Kira took the tissue he offered and wiped her eyes.

"No worries. I can handle a few tears." He took her right hand in his, being careful of her gauze bandages. "It would be weird if you weren't crying. You and Michael had a special bond when you were kids."

Kira half laughed and sniffled at the same time. "Remember that time you two went drag racing out on Jefferson Road? And you put Aunt June's car in the ditch?"

Lukas laughed and leaned forward on his elbows. Sunlight streaming through the kitchen window rimmed his hair in reddish-blonde highlights. Her stomach clenched as pain throbbed over her right eye. For a second, she could smell the French fries in their high school cafeteria. Was that from her concussion?

"I was terrified of her, but I knew I couldn't leave him alone to take the fall." His thumb gently caressed her right wrist. "She made us pay off the towing bill by cutting her grass for the whole summer. And your neighbors, the Sundstroms'. That sure kept us out of trouble."

"I don't know who was more of a bad influence, you on Michael or Michael on you." Her stomach churned as she put her hand to her forehead.

"Oh, definitely him on me. Michael always cooked up some scheme to keep us busy after youth group." He paused. "You all right, there?"

Kira's lower lip trembled. She took a breath and nodded. "Why didn't I take the time to email him? Or text him?" More tears fell, and she held another crumpled tissue to her eyes. Sophie came over to her and put her arms out.

"Up? Up?"

"Come here, baby," Lukas said. "Don't bug Kira." He hugged Sophie and smooched a kiss on her cheek, then pointed her towards her coloring book and crayons.

"She's okay," Kira said. "At least she's not scared of me. I must look horrifying between these burns and bandages."

"You are many things, darlin', but horrifying is not one of them." He stood up from the table and piled their dishes on the counter.

Kira blew her nose.

"Although, you made short work of that guy the other day." He turned away from the counter and leaned against it, folding his arms across his chest. "Where did you learn those moves?"

"Self-defense class." She cleared her throat. "Every woman needs to know how to defend herself. Although, I only have my green belt in Taekwan-Do."

"Only your green belt?" Lukas laughed as he returned to the table with a brand new box of gauze and a tube of antibiotic ointment. "Isn't that one level below a black belt?"

"It's two levels below a black belt," said Kira as he sat down and pulled on a pair of one-use first aid gloves. "When did you have time to get all of this stuff?"

"Ruby picked it up for me." Lukas gently pulled her hands towards him and turned them palm up so he could unwind the gauze strips on her right hand. "You need this changed daily, and we need to keep an eye out for infection." She winced at the gauze as it tugged on her skin. "Sorry," Lukas said. "I'm trying to go easy."

Her fingers on her right hand were redder from touching her room key. Her palms had caught the brunt of the fire flash as she'd thrown her hands up in a defensive move. Lukas concentrated on easing off the gauze on her left hand, his fingers unwinding the bandages as if tending to a baby bird.

Kira watched him from under her lowered eyelids. This moment of silence between them felt safe. His tender touch soothed her nerves as well as the burned skin on her palms.

"There," Lukas said as he finished dabbing on the antibiotic ointment with a cotton swab. "This should do it. No sign of infection and this non-stick dressing on the back of your hands should help speed up the process, too." He wrapped the gauze loosely around her hands and tucked the ends in. "In another day or two, we can see how your fingers are doing and leave them free."

He let her hands go, and the spell of the moment was broken. Kira gave herself a shake.

She pushed her chair back and stood. "Can I borrow your phone? I'd like to give my boss a quick call."

"Talking, no texting." Lukas moved the first-aid products to the counter. "It's on the living room table."

Kira punched in the phone number as her thumbs were the only parts of her hands not covered in gauze.

"Birchall." The answering voice was clipped.

"Professor Birchall, it's Kira."

"Kira? Where are you? I went over to the health centre, and they said you'd been discharged."

"I'm... staying with a friend. I might not get out to the Wildlife Management Area to check the DNA traps with Eva for a day or two. Can Ross go with her? I don't want the project to stall just because I'm... unwell."

"Unwell? I thought you were seriously injured. Which is it?"

"Okay, I'm injured. But concussions can sometimes heal quickly. The burns will heal in about a week."

"I need you back before then. And when is your room going to be released? The cop locked it and said some forensics ident tech has to go over it."

"I have no idea. How much damage was there? I need to get some clothes."

Professor Birchall snorted. "Your room is destroyed—just what we needed. An insurance claim." He sounded beyond irritated. "First your brother and now you. You're both more trouble than you're worth. Misfortune must run in the family."

Kira gripped the phone so hard pain shot up her wrist. *First your brother...?* What a lousy thing to say, even for her boss, who was known to be a crank.

"The cops removed stuff from your room after the fire. Why? Is it evidence of arson?"

Say something! What's wrong with him? Her sarcastic brain had a saucy comeback, but she needed this job.

"I have no idea," she said. "No one's told me anything."

"Can I get you at this number?"

"Yes, this is Lukas Tanner's phone. Please let me know if any of my clothes are still wearable." Although, "destroyed" probably meant that was a big, fat *NO*.

Professor Birchall was quiet for a few seconds. "You can call back." He hung up.

She put the phone down. No one liked insurance claims, but she'd hardly set fire to her own room. Still, Professor Birchall was known for his impatience and perfectionist tendencies. He was a scientist, but he had an "artistic temperament," according to his grad students. Despite how difficult he made it, she worked hard for him.

Misfortune must run in your family.

Sophie banged a spoon on top of the plastic tote Lukas had brought back with them. Kira stared at it. All of Michael's personal effects from his desk and dresser were in that tote. Was Lukas right? How much of a coincidence was it she'd been attacked right after the funeral?

She went over and bent down to Sophie's level.

"Hey, sweetie, can I see that box, please?"

Sophie graced her with a huge grin and pushed the tote towards her. Kira picked it up between her forearms and carried it to the kitchen table. Her breath hitched in her chest, and she paused so it would slow down. She eased off the semi-melted plastic top, stared inside, and frowned.

A couple of framed family photos had melded with the plastic side of the tote. Michael's watches were in velvet boxes. Her throat tightened, and unshed tears choked her. His favourite watch in its blue box sat in a hunk of melted plastic from the tote. Could it be saved? She pulled out the other watch boxes and set them aside.

"Oh." She scooped up a figurine with both hands, careful of her bandages. "It's barely touched." She hugged it to her and sat in the chair. Then the tears came. Sobs flowed from deep within as she held a carved wooden owl statue. Lukas came over to her side.

"Michael made me this in woodworking when we were in high school." Scorch marks rode up the wood on the owl's back and head, but it was in one piece.

Lukas rubbed her shoulder while she turned the statue over and over in her hands. "I remember this," he said. "He hand carved it and used rose quartz for the eyes."

Kira smiled up at him through her tears. "I'd left it behind on a visit. I can't believe he kept it all these years." She turned it over and rubbed the black marks. The left wing moved. "That's not supposed to happen." She tugged, and the wing slid forward, leaving a hole. She put her left index finger inside and gasped. "There's something in there."

She held it over her left hand and shook until an orange flash drive fell onto her bandaged palm. "64G" stood out on the top; otherwise, there were no identifying features.

"Why'd he put a flash drive inside it?" Lukas asked.

She turned the flash drive over twice in her hand and shrugged. "It was on the bookshelf in his bedroom, tucked behind some books. If I hadn't been sorting them, I'd have missed it, but he made it for me, so I wanted to keep it."

"So, is this something from a long time ago, or do you think he wanted to keep the flash drive hidden?"

"I won't know till I check what's on it," she said. Her heart beat a tattoo against her ribs again. Michael had been ultra neat and organized to the bone, with the same sharp, scientific mind she had. He'd never have forgotten where he put something. That meant he'd hidden it. She squeezed her fist shut around the flash drive, ignoring the pain.

You and your brother are more trouble than you're worth.

Really? Anger choked her. Her room destroyed, her brother's memories destroyed, her brother–*oh, Michael!*–her brother dead.

Kira stared up at Lukas. "Laptop. Now."

45

CHAPTER 5

Lukas ushered her to a black laptop on his desk in the living room, then stepped back as if to get out of the range of explosion. Kira sat down and booted up the computer. She was rigid, and her bandaged fingers stabbed at the keys to no effect. Her headache throbbed a few levels higher. She smashed her hands down on the keyboard.

"Argh!"

"May I?" Lukas put his hand over hers, bringing them down to her lap. Tears overflowed, running down her cheeks again. Lifting her hands in surrender, she vacated the desk chair and walked away, her back to him. She crossed her arms and clutched her sides, trying to hold in her temper.

"It's password protected," Lukas said, pointing to the USB stick.

She grimaced. What now? She walked back to the desk. She suggested their childhood nicknames, places they'd lived, and their birthdates. Nothing. Then she suggested Jasper, the name of the one beloved dog Aunt June had let them adopt from the humane society. The flash drive files opened, and Lukas clicked on the email folder.

Three pages of financial statements showed deposits and withdrawals between several accounts and a list of emails dated over the past three weeks. She leaned over and clicked on the most recent one.

Date: Friday, October 26, 2018
From: Stan Johnson, VP Tedford Mines
To: Alison Webster
Re: Company 36289

Due to weather restrictions in the area, all activity will cease within two weeks. Need another suitable site, so you need to advise asap. All costs incurred will be your responsibility.

Reminder that Webster Technologies owes us $10 million as of your husband's recent death. We're happy to provide this waiver should you solve our immediate problem above.

S. Johnson

Kira clicked on the next several emails. They had the same subject line and used the same cryptic language. They were to and from the same people, although Alison Webster never replied. It seemed Michael had kept just the emails from Stan Johnson of Tedford Mines.

Date: Friday, October 12, 2018
From: Stan Johnson, VP Tedford Mines
To: Alison Webster
Re: Company 36289

Moving three parcels within twenty-four hours. Make sure delivery is met with proper assistance.

And on Friday, October 5, 2018, an email read, "Moving five parcels within forty-eight hours. Delivery will need security."

Kira stood back after skimming the list of emails, all from Johnson and all except the most recent referencing "parcels."

"What do you make of these?" she asked. "What 'parcels' would a mining company be delivering? And what kind of security are they talking about?"

"Your guess is as good as mine," he said. Lukas twisted in the chair and put his hand on her arm. "Michael must've known what these companies are, but I have no idea what's going on."

He removed his hand, and, once again, she felt the loss of his warmth.

"Maybe you should ask his boss, Alison Webster, if you run in to her again."

"I guess I could," she replied. "She seemed concerned about Michael's death."

Lukas cocked his left eyebrow. "She seemed pushy and ostentatious, but whatever." He turned back to the computer. "She'll know the answers because the emails were sent to her. And she owes this mine ten million dollars; that's not chump change."

"I still can't see what this has to do with Michael. He would never do something dishonest. If these emails weren't meant for him, I don't know why he has them." Kira paced back and forth. She put her right hand to her temple and scowled. "How long before I can take another pain pill?"

He jumped up. "You should sit or lie down. I'll get your pills." He pointed to the couch. "Sit, please. You look like you're about to fall over."

She sank on to the couch and leaned her head back. It hurt to think even if Lukas was bossing her around again.

Relax, he's just looking out for you. You're a bad patient at the best of times. But this headache! God, could you please make it end?

Sophie crawled up on the couch beside her carrying a large book.

"Hey, would you like me to read to you?"

Sophie's smile and giggle lit up the room. She threw herself at Kira, climbing up on her lap, waving the book back and forth.

"Let's try this way." Kira maneuvered the child sideways on her lap. She put her arms around Sophie, who leaned back and put her thumb in her mouth. "What a nice book." Kira smiled. "*Green Eggs and Ham* by Dr. Seuss."

She read the familiar verses, growling out the rhyming words, which earned her more giggles from Sophie as she used her index finger to draw lines under the words.

When they finished, Kira asked, "Can she read, then?"

Lukas folded his tea towel on the counter.

"No, she's just copying Ruby. Ruby believes repetition will help her learn to read."

Sophie edged off Kira's lap, ran over to a bookcase, and grabbed another book.

"You've started something now," Lukas said. "And you're not supposed to be reading, either, the doc said."

Kira smiled. "It's big print. I think I can handle it." She pulled Sophie up into her lap. "Okay, let's read."

"One more story, Soph. Then Kira has to talk to Daddy, okay?" He wiggled his eyebrows at his daughter. Sophie put her arms around Kira's neck and hugged her. "Don't go choking our guest now," Lukas said. "But seriously, Kira, we need to talk."

"Okay, Daddy, we're almost done."

Kira settled Sophie down and began reading.

Lukas finished loading the dishwasher and watched his daughter lying with her thumb in her mouth, on Kira's lap, listening to the story. Sophie didn't remember Abby even though he had several photos of the two of them in Sophie's bedroom. What three-year-old would remember a mother gone so soon? And with her delayed development, would she ever understand who her mother had been or even what death meant? So many questions, and he had no answers.

But he couldn't allow Sophie to get emotionally close to Kira the way she was with Ruby, because Kira was a scientist who would leave when her project finished. Would he have the strength to let that happen again? Probably not. The best thing for him and Sophie was to keep his heart guarded and secure.

He headed over to them, clapping his hands. "Hey, girls, how about we go feed the dogs? They've been so patient while we've been lazing around in here." He plucked Sophie from Kira's lap and swung her around in a circle, earning him more giggles.

"Sounds great," Kira said. "I'll grab my parka."

Lukas bundled Sophie up in her toque, scarf, and snowsuit before Kira had finished wrapping her scarf around her own face. Sophie grabbed his cell phone from the hall table and sat on the floor playing with it. She held it out to Kira, pointing to a red dot with a red circle around it, saying, "Me, me, me."

"What's this?" Kira asked. "Are you on Daddy's phone?"

"Yes'm, me here." Sophie hitched herself up onto her knees and gave Kira the phone.

"That's her Little Lamb tracker" Lukas said. "I've got one in all her boots, shoes, backpacks, outdoor wear, etc."

"What's a Little Lamb? I'm not up on kids' accessories."

Little girls' fashion might not be his thing, but technology? This would be fun to show off. Lukas headed to the desk in the living room and returned with a quarter-sized piece of metal. "Here, give me your boot."

Kira handed over her right boot. He pulled up the insole and deposited the circle of metal underneath it, smoothing it down again.

"It's so thin you won't feel a thing. Then I bring up the app on my phone..." He punched in a few numbers. "Put in your name, and voila, you're on the map on my phone." He showed Kira. "Now I'll never lose either of you." He grinned.

The millisecond of alarm in her eyes made him step back. *Whoa! Sensitivity overload!* He ducked his head to give himself time to recover.

Kira put her boot back on. "You're right. I don't feel it at all." She wiggled her foot back and forth. "Are they expensive?"

"Some people might think so. For Sophie's safety, I don't count the cost. It's only good up to a mile, according to the warranty and directions. But you can use them on anything. The dogs have them on their collars, too."

Embarrassed, he shoved his feet into his own boots, picked up Sophie, and headed out the side door. Gunner burst past them, leaping off the deck and running circles in the crystalline snow.

Their breath made frosted clouds in the frigid air. The never-ending breeze wafted snowflakes through the air in swirls of white across his property. Sophie laughed as she stuck out her tongue to catch them. No pollution, no industrial smells. Just fresh, tingling air. Lukas sighed with contentment as their boots crunched across the new snow covering the frozen ground.

"The barn has everything we need," he spoke over his shoulder. "I've got a freezer and fridge in there because I feed them a raw diet."

Kira hurried to catch up. "So, these are working dogs, right? Not pets?"

"They're working dogs, but I still treat them like family. They stay out here in the barn at night." He grinned. "Why, did you think I'd have nine dogs in the house all the time?"

The barn smelled of sawdust. He let Sophie down, and she waddled over to a plywood gate across an open box stall where the huskies jumped up and barked. Showing no fear, she reached her mittened hands upwards, trying to touch their noses and giggling. The dogs yipped and rested their front paws on top of the gate with tongues lolling, their eyes bright.

Several box stalls ran down this side of the barn. The other side was open and held shelves of dry dog food, medicines, and two more dog sleds.

"You don't have to change your routine on my account." Kira shut the barn door and joined him at the counter by the fridge. A window over the sink let in a shaft of brilliant sunlight, but he flicked on an overhead electric light to illuminate the kitchen area.

He pulled plastic containers of meat out of the fridge and picked up a stack of bowls from the floor.

"Here." He handed her nine bowls. "Just put two hunks of meat in each one, and we'll put them in a circle over here." He indicated the center of the room. "You can use a fork if you don't want to touch the meat."

Kira raised an eyebrow. "Please, do you have any idea of the kinds of things I touch in my line of work?"

She picked up a long-handled fork and set of tongs from the counter. "Mind you, I do tend to use gloves for the yucky stuff."

She dumped pieces of half-frozen meat into the bowls. "What kind of meat is this?"

"Caribou. Sometimes friends farther south will ship me frozen deer or moose. I feed raw because it keeps them strong for sledding." He swept Sophie up in one arm and opened the plywood gate with the other hand. "Here you go guys. Circle!"

The dogs halted midstride, and each one planted its haunches in front of a bowl in the circle, watching for the next command. When each dog had its eyes on him, Lukas said, "Take it!"

They all dove into the meat, chowing down with gusto. Kira laughed.

"They sure appreciate your choice of food." She shoved her bandaged hands in her parka pockets. "Where did you get them?"

"One's from my uncle's original team, but the others are rescues. Male and female, but I had them all fixed." He smiled at her. "I'm not in the breeding biz. Not enough time in the day."

Sophie squirmed forward and pointed at the largest dog, a black and white husky with one blue eye and one brown. "Ti-brrrr!"

Lukas hugged her. "Yeah, sweetie, that's Timber. Good talking! He's the lead sled dog." He pointed to Timber and then around the circle, clockwise, for Kira's benefit.

"That's Timber, Shala, Magnus, Valour, Tessa, Apollo, Max, and Remy. Timber and Gunner are the only ones we named. The others all came with a name."

"Can I pet them?" Kira moved closer to the circle.

"Not till they're done eating. That's the rule, right, Soph?" He jiggled Sophie on his hip. "And Sophie's never left alone with any of them. They're 'pets' because I treat them well and we love them, but they're prey driven, and it's their nature. Better safe than sorry."

Kira put up her bandaged hands. "Hey, I totally agree. Too bad she doesn't have one to cuddle with though." She blushed again. "Sorry! None of my business."

"Gunner's a guard dog, but he's devoted to her. Can you hold her while I clean up?" He held Sophie out to her.

"Sure." She lifted Sophie on her hip. "Maybe we should take a walk outside."

"Stay close to the barn," Lukas said. "I'll be just a minute."

And not a second later. If Kira was a walking disaster magnet, he needed to be one step behind. After all, she carried his entire world in her hands.

Kira hefted Sophie higher on her hip before she closed the barn door. "Okay, let's see if we can find something fun to do."

She walked around the corner of the building, her boots crunching on the crisp snow. The flawless, blue sky made a perfect dome overhead. The snow dazzled in the sunlight, and she could see straight west across the tundra to the outskirts of the town's buildings.

"Look, Sophie! Birds flying that way." Kira pointed to the sky. Sophie clapped her hands in delight.

Glancing down, Kira halted and swayed on her feet. Animal track imprints crossed in front of her. Prints that were twelve inches across, with the familiar five points of three-inch-deep claw marks. Those claws were strong enough to drag a one-hundred-fifty-pound seal out of a hole in the ice. Or tear muscle from bones. She gasped and hugged Sophie tighter. She slowly turned in a circle. Nothing but flat open snow as far as she could see.

"Lukas!" Her throat felt like sandpaper, and her call came out in a squeak. She cleared her throat and shouted again.

The barn door banged, and he skidded around the corner.

"Stop! Do you see them?" Kira flexed her hand out in the universal sign for *stop*.

"See what?"

She pointed down and then along the path of the tracks heading towards the house. "Polar bear tracks. I can't see a bear though."

Lukas made it to her side and took Sophie in one motion. "Take my hand. Don't walk too fast, but keep up a good pace." He headed back towards the barn. "I'll get my shotgun and cracker shells from the locked cabinet in the spare stall. You two stay in here till I make sure it's clear to the house."

She nodded and grasped his hand. Normally, she was in the ASCR's Arctic Rover. Thirty-five feet long, made of reinforced steel and built to ride ten feet off the ground, it kept them safe when they crossed paths with a bear out on the tundra. But she'd never seen bear tracks this close to a dwelling before, and her heart pounded as hard as her headache. She breathed easier when they closed and latched the barn door.

"Be careful," she whispered to his back when he reached the locked gun cabinet. She didn't know why she was whispering. Any polar bear hanging around would already have picked up their scent or seen them outdoors. She knew that the bears' eyesight was the equivalent of humans. Their predatory instincts made them excellent hunters. Lukas going back outside alone was begging any bear within a kilometer to run him down. This was the old Lukas she remembered, the one who'd run into danger without a second thought.

She held Sophie close as he took down the box of cracker shells and loaded his shotgun. He also grabbed a small air horn off the counter. She saw cans of bear spray lined up across the back counter. It must be her headache because she hadn't noticed before how many bear deterrents he had in the barn.

With the shotgun cradled in his right arm, he dropped a kiss on Sophie's hat and hesitated a second before placing a brief kiss on the top of Kira's head as well. Her face flushed, and, impulsively, she pulled him closer and brushed a quick peck on his cheek.

Never mind that—you need to keep Sophie safe.

Lukas's voice cut through her fear. "Don't worry. Here's my cell phone. Call the Natural Resource's Office and report we've sighted tracks—it's number three on speed dial."

"You have them on speed dial? How big a nuisance bear problem do you have out here?"

Lukas turned back from the door. "I have everything on speed dial. Keeping Sophie safe is my only priority." He patted his parka pockets. "Just call and let them know. I'll sound the air horn a few times in case it's still around."

Kira grabbed his sleeve. "Be careful," she murmured. "Don't take any chances." Her heart hitched in her chest when she saw the warmth in his eyes. He rubbed his knuckle on her nose and grinned. "When I know it's safe to come out, I'll be back to get you two to the house." He headed out into the frigid air.

Kira made short work of the phone call. The natural resource's officer said to follow polar bear protocol and stay inside. *Seriously?Well, duh!* She hung up with her pulse pounding. Sophie wriggled, trying to get down.

"Hang on, Sophie. Daddy's going to blow that horn and tell us when it's clear, okay?"

For the first time, she noticed bars on all the barn windows. To keep the bears out and protect the dogs. The Lukas she'd known hated camping, yet here he was living on the edge of the wilderness, in a small town of nine hundred people, with limited resources. How had his new wife changed him so radically?

Part of me wants to know, and part of me wants to go back to The Dove restaurant and make a different choice.

She cuddled Sophie, who kept making noises and pointing at the door.

"Don't worry, sweetie. I want to see your daddy as much as you do!"

Okay God, we haven't been in touch for awhile, but if You're out there, please don't let Lukas come in contact with that bear. Keep that bear far, far away from the house and barn. Keep us all safe, the bear included. Amen.

Lukas drove his 4x4 pickup to the barn door. He hadn't seen any bears but fired off two cracker shells, one towards the front and one towards the back of his property. Their deep boom echoed across the open tundra. However, given that polar bears could run at speeds up to forty kilometers an hour if they felt like running down a human being, he wasn't about to take any chances with Sophie and Kira.

More disconcerting were the large boot prints he'd found around his garage and back deck. Size eleven snow boots, if he had to guess. Remnants of broken sticks and seal skin strips showed human hands had tied chunks of raw meat to the corner of his back deck. Blood red snow had frozen in peaks around the deck. Polar bear tracks crisscrossed the immediate area. The bear had eaten the meat and would return to find more easy pickings.

Everyone knew not to leave hunting kills outside where the smell would attract bears. Someone had deliberately planted fresh meat to do just that—bring a bear or bears right up to his house. Lukas had shoveled up the affected snow and bagged it, leaving it locked in the attached garage. He wouldn't mention the incident to Kira, but he was glad he'd brought Gunner inside last night.

When he opened the barn, Kira's face was as white as the snow packed on the ground, but she still held Sophie. She rushed over to him, her pupils wide and dark, her breathing shallow. He drew her into a side hug, brushing another kiss across her temple. Deep slashes of blue under her eyes revealed her exhaustion. She wavered where she stood. *Did I do the right thing bringing her out here with a concussion? She needs more rest.*

"I'll take love bug here," he said, "Do you need anything from the

56

house? I'm thinking we should head to Ruby's place. I've got a friend who can check on the dogs."

"Whatever you want," Kira said. "Until I get my own clothes, I feel like a bit of a nomad."

He gave Sophie a brief hug and strapped her into her car seat, patting her on the knee. "Hop in," he said to Kira. "No offense, but you look terrible. Do you want to check in at the health centre?"

She looked worse than terrible. He'd believed he could protect her out here, but he had no medical expertise. His rush to bring her home had more to do with needing to keep her both safe and near him. Now neither she nor Sophie was safe. Kira swayed on her feet and clutched the truck door handle with white knuckles. When he came around to her side, she motioned him away with her right hand.

The sound of another vehicle crunching across the snow made him turn around. Constable Koper drove the white RCMP truck up and rolled down his window. Lukas blew out the breath he didn't realize he was holding. *Thank you, Lord. I can use the back up.*

"Afternoon, folks. Thought I'd swing by and take Kira's statement here, if that's all right."

"We were just deciding whether she needs to get checked out again in town."

"I got a message from Sarah Thorvald over at the natural resource's office. You've got a polar bear out here?"

"He's gone now." Lukas glanced over at Kira to check her reaction. "The tracks are probably from last night, but this is the first time I've had a bear come so close to the house and barn."

Much as Lukas wanted to avoid Kira finding out about the boot prints and food trap, Ben could shoot to back him up if the bear circled around to see if any more meat was decorating his backyard.

"You two girls need to warm up. Let's put on a pot of coffee," Lukas said. Nodding at Ben, he got into his truck and did a three-point turn heading towards the house. Kira clutched the edges of the seat.

Lukas didn't like the pallor of her skin. "Do you even feel up to giving a report on last night?"

Kira moved her gaze from the snow outside over to him. Her pupils were dilated and her posture stiff. "I don't remember much of anything, so I don't know what good it'll do. I didn't see who hit me."

She looks shell-shocked.

"I feel stupid. I remember nothing, except the fire." The truck creaked over the ice and snow.

"Don't worry about it. Just tell him what you can. He wants to know about what happened at the cemetery, too," he said.

She hissed out a breath. "You told him about that? I thought I said I didn't want to talk about it!"

Lukas tried to control the pickup's bouncing over the ruts in the faintly marked road across the property. "I told him when you were having your CT scan. You know, it's not a coincidence you were attacked twice in twenty-four hours, in two different places spread over a thousand kilometers." He looked at her sideways. "What aren't you telling me?"

Kira bit her lower lip. "Nothing! You know everything I know."

They pulled up to the back deck. He put the truck in park and turned towards her. "Did Michael leave you a message or get hold of you on the phone last week?"

"If he did, I didn't get the message from the front desk. Why? Did he call you?" She gazed straight forward, her eyes on the horizon. "Well, why *would* he call me? We haven't spoken in more than two years." She turned towards him, her voice shaky. "What does that have to do with anything?"

"I don't know," he admitted. "Michael left me a voice mail saying he had to talk to me urgently and he'd see me this past Thursday. Sounded like he was upset about something. Something he didn't want to talk about on the phone."

"Da-Dee!" Sophie beat her boots against the back seat. "Want out! Out please!"

"Okay, okay, kiddo," Lukas said. "Let's have some cocoa, all right?"

"Yay!" Sophie trilled, waving her hands in the air.

Kira got out of the truck. Lukas watched as she put her palms to her temples and then shoved her hands into her parka pockets. She wasn't doing a great job of hiding her ongoing headache.

"What do you think Michael wanted?" Her chin tilted upwards in a determined fashion.

"Beats me," he said, releasing the five-point harness on Sophie's car seat. "Just that it sounded serious."

Kira kept quiet while he opened the back door off the deck and carried Sophie across the threshold. He figured there was nothing to gain by telling her *how* riled up Michael had been on that call. It took a lot to upset Michael. He was—had been—the most centered person Lukas had ever known. Now they'd never know what he wanted to tell them.

"You think his death had something to do with my attack?"

Lukas shifted Sophie on his hip. "I think we need the police to look at his accident again."

"Should we tell Constable Koper about the emails? I don't know—"

"Tell Constable Koper about what emails?" The police officer came up the deck stairs. Kira met Lukas's gaze, silently pleading with him to stay quiet. He shrugged and removed Sophie's snowsuit.

"You should tell him everything."

CHAPTER 6

Kira sat across the kitchen table from Constable Koper, her stomach pitching with nausea. She bit down on her thumb. It was ludicrous to be so nervous. She'd done nothing wrong. Still, this was the first time she had spoken to a police officer since her ordeal at university. She'd asked for a female cop back then, but none was available. Instead, she'd been stuck with two men, one young and exhausted from lack of sleep with a newborn and the other a detective in his fifties who'd made it clear from the start he hadn't believed a word she'd said.

"So, you think he might've had a knife? Did you see a knife? Did you cry out or yell for a friend?" He had no patience for her barrage of tears. *"Those dorm rooms have paper-thin walls. You could've screamed for help."* He had tossed a box of tissue at her, then given her a notepad and pen. *"Write it all down,"* he said. *"But if you don't remember what he looked like, we don't have a whole lot to go on."*

The problem was she knew who'd been in her room, but Derek Straughn, from her chemistry class, told her he'd return and kill her if she opened her mouth. After the filth he'd done to her, she believed him. His eyes through the slits in his ski mask—almost black—his voice a deep rasp.

Burned into her brain. After writing out her statement, she'd heard the two police officers whispering in the hall.

"She showered!" said the older guy. "Zero DNA evidence and says she didn't see his face."

"This is a total waste of time," the junior detective had said. "These girls leave their doors unlocked and wonder why they wake up and some guy's standing beside their bed."

Constable Koper, on the other hand, seemed relaxed and easygoing.

"So, Kira, we met at the health centre. How're you feeling now?"

The officer flipped open his notebook and settled back into Lukas's kitchen chair.

"Well, my head's still throbbing. And I guess it will for awhile, but these'll just take a week or so." She held up her hands to show off her palms encased in gauze.

"Okay, and why don't you call me Ben." Koper smiled, his warm, brown-eyed gaze resting on her face. He gestured at Lukas across the table. "I've known Lukas for about four years now. So, let's go back to the cemetery, after your brother's funeral—can you tell me what happened after Lukas got there?"

Kira noticed Ben's gaze on her as she played with the gold earring in her left ear. Her hand stilled, and she lowered it onto her lap and locked her fingertips together to quiet her nerves.

"We talked, and then I got into my car to leave for the airport because I was late."

Her right knee bounced under the table. Her face flushed, her sympathetic nervous system working full tilt. Lukas put a reassuring hand on her knee. She glanced at him with a half-smile.

"I know you're not going to believe this..."

"Try me," Ben said.

Kira drew in a sharp breath. "A stranger opened my driver's door. He grabbed me and yanked me out of the car."

"You'd never seen this man before?" he asked.

Kira shook her head.

61

"Was he alone? Did he speak with any kind of accent? Could you see any distinguishing marks on him?"

Her knee jumped up and down again under the table. "There was a driver, too. I didn't register any accents. I don't remember any marks or tattoos. They were Caucasian, and the one who grabbed me was taller than Lukas. About your height."

"So about six-foot-three?" Ben tapped his pen on his notebook.

"That sounds about right," Lukas said. "And the van was white. I didn't get a plate either."

"So, there's no use in looking at mug books then," Ben said to her. He scribbled in his notebook.

"Oh," Lukas added, "the back windows were blacked out, and some kind of logo was painted over."

"Well, that's something." Ben wrote faster. "Let's talk about last night. What you were doing leading up to the attack?"

Kira sat with her hands in her lap. Her skin prickled at the warmth emanating from Lukas's body beside her. He and Ben seemed to be good friends; she should be able to trust him. Without thinking, she edged a little closer to Lukas in her chair.

"I could see my clothes in flames on my bed—like a campfire." She toyed with the gauze on her left hand. "I remember getting thrown backwards when something else combusted and hitting the door frame. I didn't see who hit me." She shrugged. "That's it. I woke up in the health centre. Nothing more to tell."

Ben Koper sat still in his chair and looked from her to Lukas and back again. "Was there anyone hanging around the building who didn't belong there? Do you remember who was in at the time? Isn't there a whiteboard in the lobby where you're supposed to sign in and out?"

"I had signed back in. I don't remember anybody else's name up there, but I was exhausted. There's about thirty of us altogether out there. You could probably ask the night security staff. The only person I saw and spoke to was Eva."

"I know this is hard to think about, but is there anyone you've angered or upset lately?" he asked.

Kira shook her head. "I get along with everyone. My government work is secret, but it's not as if it affects national security." She twisted her earring again. "Neither Michael nor I have any significant money. So why someone would want to kidnap me is beyond me." She gave a shaky laugh. "I was hoping to find insurance papers in one of those boxes I brought back because I don't know how I'll pay for the funeral otherwise."

Ben's gaze on her reminded her of Michael, earnest and kind. "So, Eva said a couple of your totes were missing after the fire. Have you had time to look at what's left in the one I gave Lukas?"

She bit her lip again and looked away.

"Kira?" Ben's voice sharpened. "Was there anything relevant to your attacks?"

She swallowed. *I'm going to come off like a hysterical female.*

"I don't know if it's relevant. You'll probably think I'm worrying over nothing."

"Try me."

She went over to the desk, took the flash drive out of the desk drawer and plugged it in the laptop, then set it in front of him. She clicked on the file folder icon and brought up the emails.

"This flash drive was hidden in a wooden owl my brother made for me years ago. I wouldn't have thought anything of it, except these emails are recent." She sat on her chair. "Read them over and see what you think."

Ben scrolled through the emails, taking his time. Lukas crossed his arms and leaned back in the kitchen chair. Finally, Ben pushed the laptop away.

"These look like delivery notices. I don't see anything sinister here."

"I know, but what are they delivering? And why would Michael care about it?"

Ben shrugged. "Do you have any ideas, Lukas?"

Lukas shook his head and straightened in his chair. "Michael was meticulous. He'd left me a phone message and wanted to tell me something urgently, but I see nothing definitive here either."

"Are there security cameras at the ASRC?" Ben asked.

Okay, I'm not hysterical, I'm just seeing things that aren't there. Tears pricked her eyes. *Oh man, I want to crawl into bed and sleep for a month.*

She put her her bandaged hands to her temples. "There are cameras outside each door because of the bears. I don't know how long they keep the recordings; I think they loop over them."

"Okay, I'll check with them anyway. But until I interview the people out there, I don't have any suspects for you." Ben flipped his notebook back two pages. "Now, regarding Michael's car accident, I spoke to the investigating officer on Winnipeg PD."

Her ears buzzed. "Why? They told me everything already."

"I wanted to double-check what happened. I told Constable Royce you'd been attacked twice in twenty-four hours. So he faxed me the accident report." Ben pulled some stapled pages out of his plastic folder. "Here's the diagram Constable Royce drew of the trajectory of Michael's car." He pushed it towards her. "There were deeper skid marks on the pavement than would be reasonable for a single car rollover. By that, I mean the depth of tire rubber left on the road. See how they start in the northbound lane and cross over the center line twice?"

She peered at the diagram, her vision blurred with tears. "I'm sorry; I'm not getting what you mean."

Ben ran his finger along the curved path on the diagram box. "Michael was traveling north, but something made him swerve into the southbound lane, back to his lane, and across the southbound lane again."

"Could it have been an animal he tried to avoid hitting?" Lukas asked.

"Maybe. He'd laid on the brakes hard, which means he was speeding."

"That's possible," Lukas said. "Michael liked driving as fast as he could get away with."

Ben put his finger on the end of the black line that showed a rectangle labeled "Vehicle 1."

"Here's where he flipped into the ditch. I asked Constable Royce if there were any signs of paint transfer on the vehicle. He agreed to check it out again in the impound lot, and there were scrapes of brown paint along the driver's side he hadn't noticed before. So, he took samples and had them tested—it's from a 2017 half-ton pickup painted in autumn bronze metallic. Nine were sold in Winnipeg, and 858 of them were delivered across Canada within the past year."

"His truck could've been scratched in any parking lot," Kira said. "What makes you think it's from the accident?"

"The paint transfer was recent. They can tell by its condition, and the paint composition was the correct color," he said. "And maybe Michael liked to speed, but with the depth of rubber he laid on the pavement, trying to prevent losing control and then ending upside down in the ditch, I'm saying it looks like someone deliberately drove him off the road."

The three of them remained silent for a moment.

"His roof was crushed; that's why he couldn't get out and drowned when the ditch water seeped in the broken window." Kira's tears rolled down her burned cheeks. "He was all alone when he died." Her shoulders shook as she sobbed into her hands. Lukas pulled her chair beside him and held her in a side hug. His strong fingers massaged the back of her neck, and he passed her more tissue.

"Kira, I'm sorry, but we have to consider the possibility that the same people who were after Michael are after you now," Ben said.

"But why? I don't even know where this mine is, and I don't care about their deliveries! If they're looking for secrets, those secrets are not on that flash drive."

Lukas pulled her head down to his shoulder and hugged her again. "There are secrets in there, but we can't tell what they are from those documents." He blew out a breath in frustration. "What are the options here? Can the RCMP do any digging on those companies? Do you have anything on Tedford Mines?"

Ben shrugged. "All I know about Tedford Mines is they're a new mine that's struck gold west of here. I can check our files to see if there's ever been any criminal investigation. Something that big would've hit the newspapers though."

Kira dabbed her burned cheek with a balled-up tissue.

Lord, Michael believed in You so strongly, and I've got to believe You didn't let him die in vain. I will follow this wherever this leads.

She straightened up from Lukas's shoulder, regretting the loss of solid strength beside her. Still, a new warm core of energy flowed within her.

"I'm going to do an internet search and see what I find," Kira said. "Michael kept these emails for a reason." She closed out the file and rolled the flash drive back and forth in her hand. "I wish he'd told me what was up." Her throat constricted, and she forced herself to breathe in through her nose.

"I'd better go through the rest of his things in that box." Searing pain circled her head.

"I'll check at work and let you know what I find out about the mine." Ben flipped his notebook shut. "I'll get this typed up at the station, and you can sign it later. And, I'll call Winnipeg police and see if we can zero in on any of those 2017 trucks. In the meantime, stay with Lukas at all times."

She nodded, her arms wrapped across her chest, hugging herself. "Thank you for all your help."

Ben shrugged into his parka and picked up his fur hat from the table. He jerked his chin at Lukas. "Can I see you outside for a moment?"

"Sure." He looked at Kira, who pushed him a smidge on his upper arm.

"I'm fine. Go."

Lukas grabbed his coat and followed Ben out onto the front deck, closing the door on the freezing air.

Kira stood, her body stiff and rigid from the hour of telling her story. She watched the two men from the living room window, their breath pluming into frost feathers.

On their last date, Lukas took her to a luxury restaurant in a Victorian home, saying he wanted to celebrate the end of their exams. Kira wore the only good dress she owned. *The tiny, navy and white georgette print swirled around her hips, and the hemline flirted with her knees. She could still feel the softness of the fabric on her skin.*

Lukas showed up in an indigo suit and tie, his dress pants perfectly creased. He brought her a bouquet of pink roses whose sweet scent, along with his aftershave, drifted across the table. When they finished their filet mignon, he took her hand in both of his.

"Kira, graduation is behind me now. I have a guaranteed job, and you have only one more year of school." *His thumb caressed the top of her knuckles. And she tensed.*

No, no, no... don't ask me to marry you! I can't marry you, I'm not your perfect, darling Kira anymore...

"I love you. I've loved you for a long time. And I'm ready to be with you forever." *She snatched her hand back, her face burning with embarrassment.*

He looked bewildered. "Kira? What's wrong? I want to marry you."

For seconds, his words had hung in the air between them. Her throat constricted. Her vision tunneled as if she were seeing him through the wrong end of binoculars. She couldn't breathe, never mind speak. And she jumped up and ran out of the restaurant.

Now, she leaned against the curtains. Her behavior five years ago was unforgiveable. She'd never answered his texts, emails, or phone messages. Instead, she'd gone straight to her biology professor and asked to work as an intern on an ongoing sea-ice project up on Baffin Island that summer—as far north in Canada as she could get at the time.

For the past five years, she'd moved back and forth between Winnipeg, Churchill, and sometimes Iqaluit. She lived out of her suitcases, and it suited her fine. If she kept moving, she didn't have to process the horror of what had happened to her. Still, she was amazed Lukas wanted anything to do with her now.

Kira turned from the window to watch Sophie, curled up on the couch, asleep with her thumb in her mouth. She covered the child with an afghan and tucked her stuffed bunny beside her. This beautiful little girl might've been hers if she'd accepted Lukas's proposal. Never in her wildest dreams had she thought they would've ended up north together. The Lukas she'd fallen in love with was about to be handed an executive job in his father's sprawling company of global conglomerates.

Sophie sighed in her sleep and pulled the afghan closer. Kira took a few strands of the girl's lush hair and brushed them back from her cheek. She perched beside the toddler on the edge of the couch so she could watch her sleep.

Those guys are busy planning to take care of you, Kira. Isn't it about time you took care of yourself? Ben's right. Whoever was after Michael is after you now. Can you ask Lukas to put this beautiful child in danger for you?

A blast of cold air socked her in the head. Lukas shoved the front door shut on whirling snow and bright sun. He stomped more snow off his boots in the hall.

She put her finger to her lips to hush him.

"How long's Sophie been out?" he whispered. He toed off his boots and hung up his coat.

"About fifteen minutes. Right after you went outside with Ben."

"I want to pack up and go to Ruby's place," Lukas said.

Well, that didn't take long.

"We've only been here a day, and Sophie just fell asleep."

"I don't like that bear coming so close to the house. He's after the dogs for meat, and I don't want Sophie here if there's a bear around."

"Lukas, you live here," she protested. "And aren't the dogs safe in the barn?"

"I can't keep them shut up all the time." He bent down to pick up books Sophie had strewn on the floor. "I'd feel better if the two of you were safe in town."

"Okay, she's your daughter, so whatever you think is best is fine with me." She gathered up her tissues and dumped them in the kitchen garbage. "I'll give Alison Webster a call once we're at Ruby's. And Lukas," she turned back to him, "I'd like to help out with your next tour so I can help pay my way. You know, till this is over."

Lukas stopped in his tracks, his arm full of a sleeping Sophie wrapped in her afghan. "Kira, you don't have to *pay your way*. You're... we're... what brought all this on?"

She shrugged. "I want to help you like you're helping me. You're... being a friend." She crossed her arms across her chest, a habitual pose when she felt cornered. "And, I know... I haven't always been a good friend to you."

The silence stretched. Sophie sucked her thumb in her sleep. Lukas finally gave a quick nod and disappeared into Sophie's bedroom with her.

She shivered. The ASRC was no longer her "safe" place. It would take all her strength to figure out who wanted her dead. Maybe she'd been a victim when she was young but no more. It was time to make some moves of her own.

CHAPTER 7

R uby's café and emporium had been a landmark on Kelsey Boulevard since the 1970s. It embodied the north with its rough log construction and displays of First Nations crafts and fine artwork. Today, it teased Kira's nose with the fragrance of cappuccino and fresh-baked bread. Ruby's Café was a balm to her senses as she shut the door behind Lukas.

She headed over to the Emporium side of the building while Lukas took Sophie to the counter to see Ruby. Kira grabbed several plaid shirts and dark turtlenecks off the women's racks and a "Welcome to Churchill" sweatshirt with a magnificent polar bear head screened on the front.

In no time, she'd found jeans in her size, heavy socks, and toiletry items. Nothing said civilization like shampoo, deodorant, and a fresh, pink toothbrush. She dumped everything on the store's front counter. A young woman with violet hair and multiple ear piercings cracked her gum behind the cash register.

"How're you paying today?"

"Can you please put these on a tab? I work at the ASRC, but my living situation is up in the air right now."

The clerk folded the clothes in a pile. "Yeah, we heard all about the fire. That stinks."

"I'll be in to pay for these as soon as I get my purse back," Kira replied.

"I know Ruby won't mind," the girl said. "Take your time." She cast an appraising eye over Kira's baggy hoodie and sweatpants. "So, Lukas Tanner." She shoved Kira's new clothes into two bags. "He's pretty much this town's most eligible bachelor."

Kira took a step back. "Excuse me?" *He really is divorced? Or worse, separated?*

"Lukas. He's the guy 'most wanted for marriage' in this town." The younger woman hooked her fingers in the air like quotation marks. "How'd you manage to meet him?"

Heat raced up Kira's body. Her cheeks flushed pink. "I've known Lukas since high school." Kira grabbed another lip balm beside the cash register in desperation. "We're just friends."

"Just friends, eh?" Miss Violet Tresses snapped her gum again. "Staying all the way out at the edge of town at his place... you must like kids then, I imagine."

"Excuse me? And you are?" Kira arched her left eyebrow. She leaned forward to check the clerk's name tag. "Chelsea... do you even know Lukas and Sophie?"

The young woman thrust the bags across the counter at her. "Hey, I was just asking." She flipped her heavy bangs out of her face. "You're not exactly his type."

"His type?" Kira echoed like a parrot. *Lukas is so well known he has a type?*

"Abby was an Amazon. She could dress down a deer in an hour. Loved hunting and snowmobiling." The clerk snapped her gum again. "You look... fragile."

Fragile?

"I. Am. A. Scientist." Kira spat out the words. "I track polar bears. I tranquilize them and put satellite collars on them."

Her nemesis arched her own black-penciled eyebrow. "Oh yeah, that's right. Shooting them from a helicopter—that's real impressive, eh?"

Kira's head pounded. What a ridiculous conversation. And she was losing her end. She snatched the large plastic bags.

"Seeing as you know everything in town, again, Lukas and I are just friends. I'm confident you *won't* keep that to yourself." She had the childish desire to stick her tongue out at the girl but carried herself off without losing more of her composure.

Abby dressed her own deer? The Lukas I knew in college couldn't stand the sight of blood, never mind dead animals.

What had changed him so much? Kira gripped the plastic bags tighter. It wasn't any of her concern. Why didn't that thought bring her comfort?

Ruby was carrying Sophie up the wooden stairs at the rear of the restaurant when Kira returned. Lukas sat at the counter with a coffee and wedge of lemon meringue pie. Her heart raced. Did he know about his reputation as most eligible bachelor?

Kira's chest squeezed tight. Her eagerness to know more about Abby warred with her desire to pretend Lukas was still the identical young man she'd loved in university. She plunked down on the stool beside him.

"What's your pleasure?" he asked. "I'll bet they don't make pie like Ruby's out at the ASRC."

She stowed her bags under the countertop. "I'll have pecan if she has any."

He motioned to the boy filling the sugar shakers. "Chocolate pecan pie, please." He turned to her. "It's to die for, you'll love it. Do you want coffee or cocoa?"

"A large cappuccino, please. With an IV drip."

Lukas laughed. "A woman after my own heart."

Ruby appeared at the counter. "Sophie's playing games with my youngest granddaughter." She smiled at the two of them. "My daughter Joy is visiting for the afternoon. I don't get to see them as much as I'd like."

"I appreciate this, Ruby," Lukas said. "We were going out to the ASRC, but Ben called to say the forensics ident tech just started processing Kira's room. And then I got a call that my next group of clients is arriving today at 2 p.m., a whole day early. I'll have to figure out what the booking agents did wrong later."

Ruby patted his hand. "You know I adore that child. It's no bother at all." To Kira, she asked, "How's the pie, dear?"

Kira's mouth was full of delicious chocolate, brown sugar, and pecans, so she could only nod. Swallowing, she said, "Hits the spot perfectly." She sipped at the foam of her cappuccino, then took a large mouthful. She concentrated on the hot liquid warming her throat and stomach.

Stay focused. You need to figure out who's after you and why. Not worry about Lukas's marital status—and why he hasn't said anything about Abby.

She finished her pie and coffee in record time. "I'll change in the women's washroom," she said. "What time are your clients arriving?"

Lukas looked at his watch and frowned. "In about an hour. We've still got time."

She nodded and grabbed her bags from under the counter.

"I'll be back."

She could feel his eyes on her back as she left. She shivered. Déjà vu. Only then, she'd fled with fear and self-loathing. Now she wanted to run away from the pain of knowing he had loved someone else, and she didn't want to examine what that revealed about her.

Lukas couldn't deny the flickers of physical longing while he watched her retreat from him once again. But he had a job to do: keep her safe from whoever was trying to kill her. Michael would've expected it from him, and he'd promised himself he'd deliver.

Still, even with her injuries, her beauty made his throat close up and tied his tongue when he looked at her. And he had to get her to see Dr.

Stedman, but he'd rather take on a polar bear unarmed than bring that up again. She'd made it clear she had no desire to see the inside of the health centre.

He jumped when Ruby tapped him on his hand.

"Sorry, what?"

"More coffee?" She gave him a discerning look. "Never mind, you have time for one more cup."

"Thanks, Ruby." He blew out a sigh. "Didn't get a ton of sleep last night."

She tilted her head as she poured his coffee. "No?" She set the pot back on the burner and jerked her chin towards the violet-haired clerk perched on her stool at the cash register. "I'd keep an eye on what Little Miss Gossip over there was saying to Kira. Chelsea tends to exaggerate things."

Lukas shrugged. "Kira's too sensible to fall for gossip. Chelsea's harmless."

Ruby cocked her eyebrow at him. "A woman 'jilted' is never harmless, my boy."

Lukas shrugged off her comment. He sighed. "I didn't jilt anyone. A blind date is a blind date."

"This is all so surreal. Who could want to hurt Kira?" He pushed his pie plate away and took a sip of scalding black coffee.

Ruby rubbed a cloth over the immaculate countertop. "Maybe her brother got in with the wrong crowd. Drugs? Money laundering?"

"Not Michael. He was the one who kept Kira out of trouble in high school when she was in her rebellious phase. He had integrity in spades."

"Do you know why he was coming up here last Thursday?"

"No. It was serious, though, or he wouldn't spring for a flight up here." Lukas finished off his mug of coffee. "He wanted to talk to Kira, too. And they hadn't spoken for quite awhile."

He pushed his mug towards Ruby and swiveled on the stool, just in time to see Jonah Adams enter the restaurant side. Jonah headed straight over and clapped him on the shoulder.

"Hey, buddy. I need to talk to you."

"I'll get you a coffee," Ruby said.

"No, thanks," Jonah said, "I'm a bit short this week."

"On the house." She smiled.

"You got your pink slip?" Lukas asked as Jonah took a seat on the same stool Kira had just left.

"Yeah, the Port laid off another fifty workers this past Friday." Jonah gripped his coffee mug with both hands. "That brings it up to one hundred fifty of us, all out of work." He blew on the hot beverage. "Don't suppose you have any need for a warm body at Guiding Star?"

The Port of Churchill was privately owned by Webster Technologies. It shipped prairie grain containers to Europe and South America. In the town of nine hundred people, it was the largest employer.

So why would a mine contact Webster Tech's CEO about deliveries when it was cutting back employees at its main shipping port? Those emails made even less sense.

His friend had shadows under his eyes. Someone else wasn't sleeping well either. Being out of work wasn't something Jonah would tolerate.

"I can always use a bear monitor on tours, and, right now, the dogs need to be run once a day." He mirrored his friend and clapped him on the shoulder. "And I could use you as security out at the house, but I'll explain later. In fact," he looked at his watch again, "I've got to go meet my next tour at the airport."

"I'm ready when you are," a husky, feminine voice said.

Both men turned on their stools towards the sound. Lukas sucked in his breath at the sight of Kira standing there. She looked stunning in a pair of jean's tucked into seal mukluks, a blue and green plaid shirt that accented the teal streaks in her hair, and a white parka. A woolen, navy scarf looped around her throat several times. Kira had removed her head bandage. She'd managed to brush her hair forward over her stitches. She elevated work clothes to new heights.

"Aren't you going to be warm in all that?" Jonah asked.

She shrugged. "It's going down to -15°C, or so I heard on the radio." She smiled at Jonah. "I don't believe we've met before."

Jonah stood and towered over her. "Hey, I'm Jonah... ma'am." His dark brown eyes crinkled at the corners as he smiled.

Kira had to look up at him but shook his hand with a firm grip. "I'm Kira Summers. Nice to meet you. And please, don't call me ma'am. I'm pretty sure I'm younger than you."

Jonah smiled. "Kira it is, then."

Lukas shrugged into his own parka. "We'd better get going. I need to grab the bus to get the new group over to the Great Northern Lodge."

"When do I start?" Jonah asked.

"Today if you can," Lukas said. "I'll get these folks settled in, and we'll head out around 3:00 p.m. for the wildlife tour."

"You got it. Meet you at the lodge." Jonah nodded to Ruby and left.

Lukas took Kira's bags from her and motioned towards the door. "You sure you feel up to driving out to the airport? Maybe you should stay here and rest upstairs."

"I'm sure. I could use the fresh air."

Lukas looked at her pale face. "What about checking in with Dr. Stedman?"

"I'm fine. I need to get out to ASRC more than I need to see a doctor."

Her tone stung. *Well. Okay then. At least I tried to take care of you.*

He pressed his lips together to keep from saying the words out loud. Just because he'd had only a few hours of sleep didn't mean he had to take it out on her.

Bells jangled over the front door, and several people rushed inside. One man shouted, "Somebody! Help! There's a bear outside, and it's got the cop down." Another man yelled, "Grab a shovel—it's going to kill him!"

Lukas leapt off his stool before the men finished speaking. He charged out the door and down the stairs into the snow-covered street. Several people surrounded a huge polar bear, shouting and flailing their arms to get its attention. A woman hit the bear's shoulders with a hockey stick, trying to make it let go of Ben, who lay still on his stomach on the road.

Lukas ran back to his truck, jumped in, and threw it in reverse. He hung out the driver's window, and yelled, "Get away! I'll make it move." He could see blood spray on the snow. The polar bear's massive jaws had Ben by the upper shoulder. Lukas hit the gas and drove towards the bear to scare it away from Ben. He laid on his horn and stopped the truck by slamming on the brakes by Ben's feet. He backed up, spinning his tires on the snow, threw the transmission into drive again and plowed forward, his bumper coming within a foot or two of the bear.

The bear hung onto Ben.

Let go... let go... Please God, get it off! He's going to die!

Lukas's blood roared in his ears. *He's going to die. He's going to die.*

A natural resource's truck drove up. The driver stopped with its front bumper a few feet from the bear. Now they had it cornered. The woman with the hockey stick swung one more time at the bear, but she missed.

A female natural resource's officer jumped out of the passenger side of the truck, armed with a special rifle used for tranquilizing large game. She took aim and shot a large immobilizing dart into the bear's neck. She waved at Lukas to come forward with his truck. As he closed in, the bear dropped Ben and staggered backwards. It tried to lope away but swayed from side to side instead. After a minute of turning in circles, it took several wavering steps and sank to the ground. Lukas leapt from his truck and ran towards Ben, still unmoving on the bloodied, snow-covered road.

Where there'd been a loud chorus of shouting and shrieking minutes before, the crowd now stood silent, edged in a circle around the two natural resource's officers, Lukas, and Ben. Kira ran up with towels from the Café.

Lukas bent over Ben and tried to assess his injuries. Blood flowed down the side of his head from a scalp laceration. The right arm of his parka hung off his body and to the side at a crooked angle. "We need to get him down to the health centre. Somebody call them," he yelled, as he unzipped his parka and whipped the belt off his jeans.

He knelt beside Ben and yanked the belt tight around the upper arm several times, and then tied the ends as tight as possible to make a tourniquet. Kira handed Lukas some towels from the Café to staunch the bleeding coming from the top of Ben's shoulder.

Oh God, this is bad, really bad. You have to help him. Don't let him die, don't let him die.

"Kira, press on this and keep it there," Lukas said. Then he took Ben's face between his hands. "Hang in there, buddy. Look at me... just look at me."

No response.

"Ben. Ben, can you hear me?"

The male natural resource's officer ran back to his truck and opened the rear doors on his 4x4 cab. "I need a hand, guys." He waved at the two nearest men. "Let's load him up."

The men lifted Ben onto a blanket and maneuvered him onto the back seat of the truck. One of them took the remaining towels from Kira and hopped in with him to continue putting pressure on his shoulder wound. The natural resource's officer put the truck in drive and headed up to the health centre.

"We've got you, Ben," Lukas said under his breath as he watched them drive away. The health centre was a three-minute drive, at the north end of town. *Please, God, do not let him die. I cannot lose someone else.*

CHAPTER 8

K ira stood beside the redheaded natural resource's officer and stared at the drugged polar bear. It was a full-grown adult male and much larger than the one that had left tracks out at Lukas's place. Kira estimated it weighed about nine hundred to a thousand pounds. It didn't have a satellite collar because only females were tracked in the project. A male polar bear's neck grows to the same width as its head, making it too wide to accommodate a collar.

"Hey. I'm Sarah Thorvald." The officer held out her hand. "We haven't met. I'm brand-new up here."

She shook Sarah's hand. "I'm Kira, I work out at the ASRC. Great shooting! This guy should sleep for a few hours."

"Thanks. When we heard it was a human attack, I hit him up with 15 ml of Zoletil instead of 10 ml. I've radioed for the bear truck, and we'll get him over to Polar Bear Jail. This is our third one in town this week."

"How many do you have in the jail?" Kira asked.

"Six right now. We're just waiting for some new parts for the helicopter before we take them out to the ice off the Prince of Wales Fort. It's finally thickening up enough to hold the bears."

"How are so many getting through the culvert traps on the town perimeter?" Kira asked.

Sarah shrugged. "They're baited with seal meat, as always, but I guess the bears are eager to get through to the live seals on the shore ice. Who knows?"

"I should come out to the jail to check on the bears' satellite collars. Do you know how many have them on?"

"Not offhand, but you're always welcome." Sarah squatted down beside the bear to check his breathing.

"I'll try to swing by tomorrow if I can," Kira said. "Do you need any more help?"

"Thanks, we're good. Go see your friend if you like." Sarah turned away and spoke into her radio clipped to her collar.

Kira's legs trembled from her adrenaline rush until they were knocking together. She backed up till she could sit on the Café stairs where she pulled in deep breaths to draw oxygen back to her extremities.

Lord, please look after Ben. Let him be all right and survive this without too much loss of blood. Please, please, let him be okay.

She bent her head on her hands and squeezed them to stop their shaking. She *loved* polar bears. Still, they were the top of the food chain and predators. She'd never seen the damage they could do to humans.

Lucas startled her as he sat down on the stair beside her. He put his right arm around her shoulders, brushing back her hair.

"You okay?" he asked.

Kira nodded. "This is climate change. Sea ice's melting so fast the bears go hungry longer. And the winter ice doesn't freeze as fast as it did even ten years ago, so now we've got bears roaming around humans, looking for food." She shivered.

"I'm scared for Ben. He could have permanent damage to his arm or head." She leaned in to Lukas's shoulder. "It's not the bears' fault the town is built right on their migratory path out to the sea ice. But why did this one attack Ben? And in the middle of the day?"

She shook her head and gave him a tremulous smile. "I'm good. It was just—a shock. I've never seen an actual attack on a person. My bears spar with each other out on the tundra, away from humans." She wiped her eyes, and Lukas handed her a tissue.

"Your bears?" Lukas's blue eyes twinkled. "Your very own, personal bears?"

She gave him a shove. "Yes, my very own personal bears." She leaned in to him as he laughed at her. "You're a goofball."

"Well, if that's the case, I'm a lucky goofball."

"How so?"

"Because I have my very own, *personal* polar bear expert coming on my next wildlife tour. My clients will be delighted." He hugged her around the shoulders and bent down to peer at her face. "I called Jonah while you were talking to that redheaded gal. He's gone to the airport to pick up the tour group in the bus. He'll take them to Great Northern Lodge for me."

Lukas patted her shoulder once more, then stood up, holding out his hand. "What do you say we take a quick trip to the health centre? I can't go see clients until I'm sure Ben's doing all right. And, I'd feel a lot better if you got someone to check you out for your concussion status."

She sniffed back her tears and nodded. Standing, she took his hand as they walked to his truck.

"I can't tell you how brave that was, what you did," Kira said while walking towards the truck with Lukas.

"Thanks, darlin', but I was in the truck. Pretty good bear protection."

Darlin'. His old nickname for her again. Warmth that had nothing to do with her parka spread through her.

"I've heard of polar bears tearing off truck doors. Smashing and ripping off windshields. Why do you think our Arctic Rovers are so high off the ground?"

Lukas helped her up into the truck and kissed her hand before coming around to the driver's seat. He hopped in and turned over the engine.

"Sorry, I should've asked if you're okay to go check on Ben?" he asked as he pulled away. "I don't want to upset you more."

"Thanks for that, but your best friend getting mauled by a polar bear trumps my queasy stomach. I'll be fine."

She put out her left hand and squeezed his forearm as they drove away.

Lukas had acted without thinking of the danger to himself. He'd charged in to save his friend, and hopefully, he'd succeeded. She put her hand back in her lap and gazed out the passenger window. If she looked at him right now, there'd be no way she could hide her unresolved feelings for him. But she and Lukas were in the past. She needed to keep telling herself that, or she was lost.

Four hours later, Ben was still in surgery and had lost a lot of blood. The operation to repair his shoulder and stop his arterial bleeding was still touch and go. But he was alive.

Lukas had canceled the tour out to the Wildlife Management Area because the weather had turned, and snow whipped across the bay, making visibility poor. They could be socked in for a couple of days; it was hard to tell. The weather was capricious this time of year.

The scent of broiled Arctic char, roasted elk, and deep-fried potato wedges enticed Lukas into the Great Northern Lodge restaurant. Christmas music played in the background, and the lodge's huge floor-to-ceiling Christmas tree sparkled with multicolored lights and gold ornaments. The tide of voices from the laughing, excited guests sailed over him.

He pressed up against the log wall for a second, searching the crowd for Kira and Sophie. He rolled his shoulders, trying to ease the muscle tension giving him a headache. Exhaustion overrode his hunger.

He spotted Kira by the back window, snowflakes whirling against it like a ballet. She made a swooping motion with her arm, bringing Sophie a bunch of fries towards her ketchup. Kira made airplane noises when she scooped up ketchup with the fries, and Sophie giggled and threw her head back laughing. Then she reached forward for another fry, jabbing it in the pool of ketchup. His chest tightened at the sight of them together.

He'd never considered himself an emotional guy until Sophie's birth. Counting those twenty, perfect, little fingers and toes had driven him to tears for the first time since his mother died.

Raising Sophie meant experiencing life through her eyes. He'd learned patience and to enjoy the small pleasures of butterflies, birds' eggs, and birthday cake. She was a precious gift. Kira'd only been with them two days and a night, and already Sophie was passing food back and forth with her, rolling from side to side in her booster seat, laughing back as if it were Ruby eating supper with her. They looked as though they were mother and daughter already.

He shook his head to clear his vision. *Already? What's wrong with you? This is temporary. Sophie loves everyone; you have to protect her from getting too attached.*

Why had Kira fled from him in that restaurant five years ago? He'd never know the answer. She'd made no reference to their past relationship since he'd found her in the cemetery.

Stick to the plan. Maybe Sophie needs to stay with Ruby till we get answers from Winnipeg and figure out who's after Kira.

His throat tightened watching the two of them giggling and mopping up the last of the ketchup on their plates.

Kira had broken his heart the way only young love could. She'd been beautiful and wild. He found her outlook on life unusual, coming as she did from a non-Christian family. She'd questioned everything he'd grown up believing about God. In his family, everyone believed what his parents believed. And their parents before them. Period. In youth group, Pastor Hines had fielded her outrageous remarks with humour, doing his best to keep her in check, but her sharp intelligence had made even him scramble through his Bible for answers.

Lukas had admired her sarcastic wit, used to being at the top of the class. She'd been game to try any physical challenge he and Michael had come up with, even drag racing them along Jefferson Street in her best friend's car. But the night she'd prayed to accept Christ, he'd thought he'd never love anyone the way he loved her.

As he stood against the far wall of the restaurant watching Kira, reality punched him in the chest. He was still angry she hadn't answered his texts and emails back then, and angry she had acted these past few days as though they'd never been in love at all. Part of him wanted to demand answers, and the other part wanted to protect her and love her.

Love her?

So she can break your heart again? And is it her fault I never got over her? She needs my help and protection—that's it.

Lukas took a deep breath and moved through the crowd. His clients turned in their seats to chat with him about the tour. New faces also sat at the long table, and while he shook hands and fielded questions, he scoped them out against his memory of the two attackers in the Winnipeg cemetery. No single men were in this tour group, just two couples and a small family. A nice, manageable group of seven people.

He maneuvered his way to the back of the restaurant and sat down at the table with Sophie and Kira, leaning over to tickle Sophie on her neck.

"How's my Sophie doing?"

"I hope you don't mind," Kira said, "but I begged Ruby to let me take her for supper."

"It's no problem."

"She's eaten her whole dinner, and she wants chocolate cake for dessert."

"Oh, she does, does she?" Lukas laughed and kissed Sophie on her cheek. "Well, I guess we could have one tiny piece, because right after this, you're going to bed."

"So, we're staying here tonight, then?" Kira asked.

"No, I'll take you girls back to Ruby's place. I'll stay there, too, because the lodge is booked solid." He flushed. "Sorry, I shouldn't refer to an award-winning scientist as a *girl*."

The sweet sound of her laugh warmed him all over, despite himself. Her eyes no longer looked haunted but sparkled with life. "I have only one award to my name, and I'm happy no one is calling me *ma'am* in my profession." She reached across the table and clasped his hand. "I'm not ready to be that old and responsible!"

The touch sent a frisson of energy through his arm. He turned his palm over to grasp hers, but she drew away and pressed her lips together. So, she couldn't even bear to touch him? He swallowed and forced himself to smile.

Sophie kicked her heels against her booster chair in excitement as the waitress brought over a piece of chocolate layer cake. Lukas thanked her and cut the wedge into two precise pieces. He transferred one piece to another bread plate and passed it to Kira.

"Is their baking as good here as it is at Ruby's?" she asked.

He gave a halfhearted laugh. "Nobody's baking is as good as Ruby's. But every restaurant tries hard to match her. The three main restaurants here are part of the entertainment package." He wiped a splotch of chocolate off Sophie's cheek. "But I don't have to tell you that. You've been up here for months now."

He knew he sounded irritable, but his fatigue clouded his emotions. As much as he longed to delve further into her job and what Michael had been hiding, weariness dragged at his muscles and rooted his feet to the floor.

Kira stared at him with a bemused expression. He was too tired to figure out what she was thinking. He longed to tuck Sophie in bed and crash in front of an aimless television comedy show. Time to get moving to Ruby's place.

"Lukas, may I ask what happened to your wife?"

His chest tightened. He gave Sophie the remnants of chocolate icing on a spoon to buy time. *Now* she wanted to talk about their lives? Kira sat still, her hands folded in front of her on the table. He gazed into those deep, hazel eyes—was that empathy he saw there? But Kira hadn't been living here when Abby had died even though the whole town knew the story of that terrible New Year's Eve.

Lukas cleared his throat to give him another couple of seconds to regroup. He pulled out a few crayons and a napkin so Sophie could color. "We were at a New Year's Eve party two years ago. A bunch of us went snowmobiling. We wanted to bring in the new year by watching the Northern Lights." He paused, the memory of Abby thrown into a

85

heap in the snow fast forwarding in his mind. "We'd gone down to the beach. Abby got ahead of me. She went a little out of bounds, into the rocky area... She lost control."

His stomach churned. So he still had emotions to process here as well. "Abby broke her neck vertically, and they operated to fuse the two vertebrae together..." He took a deep breath to calm his stomach. "It might've worked, but then she had a brain hemorrhage and was in a coma for several days. She never woke up... she died." *He'd never gotten to say goodbye.* He forced himself to look into Kira's eyes again. "Everyone was great —Sophie was just turning a year old, and I needed a ton of help. And," he blew out a breath, "the town rallied and gave me all the help I needed."

Kira dropped her gaze to the tablecloth and fiddled with her napkin, shredding it into tiny pieces with her fingertips. "I'm so sorry, Lukas," she said. "I didn't know if I should ask Ruby because I didn't know if maybe you were..."

"Divorced or separated?" Lukas folded his forearms on the table. "I think you know me better than that."

Kira's napkin sat in a pile of paper snow. She kept her gaze on her hands, saying, "No, I never thought—I wasn't sure if she was alive and coming back..." There was a long pause. "I'm so sorry you had to go through that... horror, and I'm so sorry Sophie won't remember her mother."

His throat closed again. He forced himself to swallow. "Sophie *will* know her mother. I will make sure of it." How much should he say about Abby? "Ruby made a scrapbook for her with pictures of us." He trailed off. "Abby didn't even get to see her first birthday. Throwing that party two months after Abby died was the hardest thing I've ever done."

Kira reached across the dinner table and took his hand again. This time, she held on to it. "I'm sorry, Lukas, it was rude of me to ask." She rubbed her thumb across the back of his hand. "But I had to know." She blushed a vivid pink as she reached for her purse and grabbed a tissue. "I know I have no right to know anything about your life here."

Now that she'd opened the door to the past, should he ask her? Was this his moment to find out the truth about why she ran out on him? Before he could form the question, Kira turned to Sophie and held out her arms.

"Come here, Sophie. Let's get your parka and boots on again. Daddy wants to take us for a drive."

Well, that settled that.

She seemed happy to skirt other topics.

"Yeah, Sophie, let's go see what Ruby's up to," he said as he stood. "Everyone's had a big day." He helped Kira pull Sophie's other arm into her coat. Kira picked up Sophie's hat and mittens from the floor beside her chair and handed them to him.

He bundled Sophie's scarf around her face to ward off the sleety snow and carried her out the door. He'd be glad to crash at Ruby's place and turn in. Glad to give in to exhaustion and sleep away the turmoil in his stomach.

They walked to his truck in silence, holding their scarves over their noses to keep out the bitter cold. The snow had stopped, and the black sky lit up with the diamond-like stars overhead. Lukas refused her help to buckle Sophie into her car seat.

What is wrong with me? I'm an idiot. Of course, he'd fallen in love with someone else. Why wouldn't he? Someone he'd had a child with—a woman well known by the town and loved by most.

Someone who trumped Kira in wilderness skills and northern living, that was for sure. She'd never shot or killed an animal in her life, and she hated fishing. Camping was only for collecting her specimens and tracking her biology projects. She was far more comfortable in the lab than the great outdoors.

It was time to accept Lukas's new reality. He'd moved on without her and never looked back. Her head pounded. That stupid concussion. And, she'd seen the hurt look flash across his face when she asked her intrusive question about Abby. She should've let him tell her in his own time.

Everything was a mess and getting worse.

When are you going to learn to keep your stupid mouth shut?

Lukas parked the truck in back of the café and took Sophie out of her car seat. He was silent while he unlocked the back door to the restaurant and held it open for Kira, then let Sophie down to waddle along in her snowsuit through the rows of tables and chairs to the stairs leading to Ruby's apartment.

Kira yanked off her parka and shoved her mitts and scarf into the arms. She tossed it up onto a clothes tree beside the door in the front apartment hallway. *Why couldn't she ever control her big mouth? Wasn't self-control one of the nine fruits of the Spirit? Something else she'd lost when God abandoned her five years ago.*

Lukas scooped up Sophie and carried her on ahead to kiss Ruby with a big smack. Was he avoiding her now?

"Bath time, kiddo." He twirled Sophie around once. "Are there towels in the bathroom?" he asked Ruby.

"Everything's in there, including her bubble bath and plastic frogs."

"Thanks, Ruby."

Sophie's laughter echoed even after Lukas shut the bathroom door. Kira stood in the hall, feeling like an idiot because she couldn't stop staring at the closed door.

"Come on into the kitchen, dear." Ruby patted Kira's arm, startling her. "How about a cup of hot chocolate?" She smiled as she pulled a chair out from the table and indicated Kira should sit down. "I think I remember that's your favorite comfort drink, right?"

The soft, buttery yellow walls of the kitchen wrapped around her like a baby blanket. She took in a quiet breath. Ruby's inherent kindness brought tears to her eyes. Why was she so emotional? The last thing she wanted was to fall apart in front of a woman who exuded strength at every turn.

Ruby poured boiling water into two porcelain teacups and brought them over to the table.

"I enjoy beautiful things and love to use them, too. These were my grandmother's. When Sophie's a bit older, I'll let her use them."

Kira ran her finger around the platinum rim of the teacup. The delicate china was black with purple roses on white around the middle. Ruby sipped her cocoa and watched Kira over the rim. Putting her cup down, she said, "You know, Lukas has been alone for a while now."

Kira's head shot up. Her face burned with embarrassment.

Ruby put her hand up. "No, I'm not trying to set the two of you up. I know you've got a past with baggage."

Kira cut off a strangled sound in her throat and gulped down more cocoa. What next?

"I knew Lukas's Uncle Henry."

Her heart beat a staccato rhythm in her chest. Ruby sat back in her chair and stared off at the kitchen window.

"He and my late husband Rob were best friends. There was nothing the two of them couldn't fix mechanically. Being a single guy, he ate pretty much every night at our café."

"I'm sorry about your husband. Was it a while ago?"

Ruby sighed. "Seven years now. Heart attack." Her eyes held sadness. "We had breakfast, and I kissed him goodbye. He and our son, Rory, went out kayaking with Henry and his tourists to see the beluga whales in July." Her eyes grew moist. "They tipped over when he had the heart attack. The tourists in the kayaks near them panicked. With all the thrashing paddles and kayaks riding over each other, Rob couldn't surface." She ran her finger around the delicate edge of her tea cup. "Rory barely survived. There was nothing anyone could do."

Now it was Kira's turn to sit back in her chair. "I'm so sorry. That's a huge loss." She closed her eyes. "I can't even imagine what that must've been like."

Ruby patted Kira's right hand. "The North is a hard taskmaster. When you live up here, you know the risks." She held Kira's gaze with her own. "Every day is precious, and the present is all we have, dear. It's pointless to dwell in the past and let it dictate what we have now."

Kira wrapped her hands around her tea cup. Sounds of Sophie

singing and giggling behind the bathroom door floated into the room.

"I'm not living in the past. I'm trying to find out what happened to my brother. And figure out who wants to hurt me. I've got a target on my back."

"I meant the past for you and Lukas," Ruby said. "He was a headstrong, young fellow when he moved up here to work with Henry." She sipped her hot chocolate. "Everything had to be perfect, and he had an opinion on everything. It didn't take long for him to learn, up here, the wilderness doesn't care about how rich you are or what a high opinion you have of yourself. Surviving in the wilderness is the great equalizer of men."

Ruby stood. "Another cup?"

"No, thank you," Kira said. "That's what I don't understand. How did Abby... I mean, how did Lukas change so much? He hated camping, even with our youth group."

Ruby checked a cupboard and brought down a plastic container of shortbread cookies. "Oh dear, I forgot all about these." She arranged some on a plate and put them on the table. "Lukas was spoiled, you could tell. He had to learn everyone up here needs each other to survive. And he learned that first winter because Henry sickened so fast with cancer there wasn't even time for chemo."

Kira took a cookie and watched Ruby as she seemed to fold in on herself.

"Lukas felt hard done by, from your breakup with him. Abby challenged him and wouldn't let him wallow around. Henry put him to some good, hard, physical labor." Ruby smiled. "I guess what I'm trying to say is, whatever happened between you two is over. Think about what you could have in the present."

"It's not that simple," Kira said. "I'm not the person I was when he fell in love with me back then."

"Honey, who is? We all change and grow; it's how the good Lord made us."

"The good Lord had nothing to do with what happened to me." She couldn't have kept the bitterness out of her voice if she'd tried.

Ruby's eyes held her gaze. "Honey, I'm sure He didn't. God may allow bad things to come in to our lives, or happen to us, but He's never the cause."

Kira swallowed and looked away. "Why didn't He help me? Why would a loving God allow something so horrible...?" She shook her head as tears formed in her eyes. Ruby reached across the table and handed her a tissue.

"Hon, I don't need to know the details. I do know this—God has never left you. You have to believe that. God meets us right where we are —it could be grief, it could be sickness, it could be our own rebellious nature."

Kira brushed away the tears with her free hand. "I wish I could believe like you do, but I haven't felt God anywhere in my life in a long time."

Ruby sat still and stared into her tea cup. "And this bad thing—does Lukas know about it?"

Kira shook her head again. "I can't ever tell him." She put her left hand over her eyes. "I just can't," she whispered.

"You don't think he'd understand? He loved you so much, Kira."

"No. His dad already wanted us to break up." She sighed. "My parents were divorced. My dad abandoned Michael and me with our Aunt June. Nothing I did was ever good enough."

"That was his dad's attitude, perhaps. But the Lukas I know would've jumped over a waterfall for you."

That brought a small smile to Kira's face. She snorted a laugh. "Except he's afraid of heights."

Ruby smiled, too, and motioned for her to have the last cookie. "You know what I mean. That boy was completely heartbroken when he came up here five years ago. He must've been crazy in love with you."

"Lukas also likes everything and everyone to be perfect. I wasn't perfect anymore." Kira traced the wood grain on the table with her fingertip. "Someone took something from me I can never get back."

Ruby opened her mouth to say something, but Sophie's wail startled them both.

"She probably can't find her Floppy dog." Ruby stood and took the plates over to the sink. "I'll go give Lukas a hand." She headed down the hallway towards the bedrooms.

Kira rinsed out the teacups. Crazy in love with her? She'd been crazy in love with him, too. But that was the problem. Crazy, young love couldn't survive the shadow of evil between them. She'd run from telling Lukas because of her shame. Her stupidity in leaving her dorm room door unlocked, allowing that monster inside. Kira knew how Lukas would feel about her lost purity.

Her headache pounded harder as tears welled in her eyes.

God, I can't live with this pain any more. I've tried to bury it. I've run as far away as I can physically, but it hurts so much. Please, take this pain away. How can I accept what happened? How can I put it behind me?

She wiped her tears away with a tea towel on the counter. The kitchen was silent. No answer from God. Well, what did she expect? A blinding light with a voice from Heaven? God had been silent for the past five years.

She turned towards the door as Sophie came barreling into the room and grabbed her around the legs. Sophie grasped a tattered, grey, stuffed animal with no eyes and only one ear.

"Up! Up!" Sophie's innocent tears squeezed her heart. *She is perfect in her imperfection.* Picking Sophie up under her arms, she received a deep hug as her reward. Sophie's thumb went in her mouth, and she put a stranglehold around Kira's neck, the stuffed animal draped down Kira's back.

"What's the matter, Sophie?" she crooned to her. "It's okay, you've got your—what is it?" She looked at Lukas, who stood in the doorway, leaning against the doorjamb with his hands shoved into his pockets.

"It's Floppy Dog. That's what she calls it. It's her favorite thing here at Ruby's, and she won't sleep without it."

Ruby appeared in the doorway. "Well, of course she can't sleep without it. Who'd want to miss out on old Rex?" She crossed her arms. "Rex is a leftover from my son, Rory."

"Can I tuck her in?" Kira asked Lukas. She jiggled Sophie higher on her hip. "Yum, you smell like strawberries, sweetie."

Sophie giggled and put her head down on Kira's shoulder, her thumb still in her mouth.

"She wants you," Lukas said. "I'll tidy up the bathroom. Then I'll be in to say prayers with her."

Say prayers with her.

Kira remembered the times they'd prayed together in his '67 Mustang in the church parking lot. Prayed over exams, summer jobs, and for friends. A sob caught in her throat. She'd run away from so much. *Because you thought you weren't perfect anymore.*

"We'll tuck in right now, okay, baby doll?" Kira hugged Sophie as they eased past Lukas. "Say, 'good night, Ruby.'"

Sophie waved at Ruby over Kira's shoulder. "Nih-nih."

"Good night, my darling," Ruby said.

Kira gently put Sophie down on the twin bed in the back room. A fairy nightlight glowed on the white bedside table. Sophie snuggled into her pillow and grasped Floppy Dog to her chest. Kira sat on the pink and white bedspread and smoothed the covers over Sophie's shoulder and chin.

Tears sprung again in Kira's eyes. She kissed Sophie's bangs and swept her light brown hair behind her ear.

I'm the one who deprived myself of a future with Lukas. I could've reported it was Derek who assaulted me. I should've been brave and taken my chances in court.

The shadow of Derek Straughn separated her life into *before* and *after*. *Before* the assault was a carefree life with Lukas. *After* the assault was a life without Lukas: A life where she'd stopped being the perfect girl for him and became someone else. Someone she believed was tainted and unworthy.

Sophie's thumb fell out of her mouth as she gave herself over to sleep. Lukas appeared in the bedroom doorway, startling Kira.

"I'm sorry, she fell asleep so fast!"

He smiled. "It's fine. We're not used to going so many places in one day."

"And it's all my fault," Kira said.

Lukas came over and lifted her chin so she had to look him in the eye. "No, it's not your fault. It's the fault of whoever's out there looking for you. Okay?"

She nodded, grateful for the warmth of his fingers against her skin. A small gesture, but it made her feel safe.

"Let's let her sleep. Do you leave the light on?"

He nodded. "She calls it her fairy-berry light. At home, she doesn't need one."

"Okay." Kira stood and took one last look at the child. "She's so beautiful, Lukas. You're lucky."

He took a step back.

"I'm sorry! Did I say something wrong?"

"No, no. I am lucky. I just... didn't think you'd think so."

Kira put her hand on his upper arm and gestured towards the door. She left the door open a crack as they left so they could hear Sophie in the night.

"Why would you think so little of me?" she whispered in the hall.

Lukas frowned. "It's not that, it's just that a child like Sophie..."

"A child like Sophie's a lot of work, dedication, and commitment. Right? Is that what you were thinking?"

"Yes. She needs dedication and commitment. Everything must be taught to her in different ways than the norm. She needs constant supervision..."

"And you don't think I'm capable of dedication and commitment?"

Lukas reached for her arm, but she yanked it away.

"C'mon, Kira, that's not what I said. I have no idea what her future holds."

Kira gasped. "One thing I've learned, Lukas Tanner, is the future is never what you think it will be."

With that, she flung herself down the hall away from him.

Oh Lukas! If only... I weren't what? Imperfect? A victim?

She had nowhere to go but fought the desire to run as far away as possible.

CHAPTER 9

The living room clock gonged 10:00 p.m. Kira woke with a start. Disoriented, she took a moment to realize she was on the couch at Ruby's apartment. She shivered in the chill of the room. An afghan seemed like a good idea, so she got up and crept to the hall closet. A prolonged buzzer sounded, and she jumped and grabbed her throat. It buzzed a second time. She whirled to reach the apartment door before it sounded again.

Eva stood on the other side, covered in snowflakes, a duffel bag over her shoulder.

"What're you doing here? Are you all right?" Kira whispered.

Eva shifted the bag. "Yes, sorry it's so late. I heard from Chelsea you guys were staying here for now." She took off her toque. "I thought you'd want to see your phone right away."

"Come in—Chelsea told you?" Kira said. "And I thought my phone was destroyed in the fire."

Eva knocked snow off her boots on the boot tray in the outside hall and toed them off. Kira took the duffel bag from her and let her in the door, putting the chain lock on after she closed it.

"No, the forensic ident tech found it near the doorway." Eva sat on the couch. "I saw her at the ASRC visiting Avery. I brought you some clothes, but not much survived."

Kira took the cell phone and thumbed it open.

"Two text messages from 'unknown' and one from Aunt June." Kira led the way into the living room just as Lukas appeared from Sophie's room. She gasped when she looked at the messages.

He yawned. "What're you doing out here? You should be in the den on the futon."

"Eva just brought me my phone and look here." She handed him the phone. "Check those out."

"This is me buying clothes downstairs at Ruby's today, and look what's written underneath it."

Lukas rubbed his eyes and turned the phone around the right way in his hand.

"We know you have it," Lukas said. He looked up. "Someone's watching you."

She crossed her arms over her chest and shivered. "Scroll down."

A photo of Lukas, her, and Sophie eating in the restaurant that night appeared on the phone screen.

"You're not the only one in danger."

Kira's knees gave out, and she sank down on the couch, her hand smothering a moan.

"We need the police, but there's no one now that Ben's in the health centre. Lukas, what're we going to do?"

He read the final text on the phone. "Aunt June says a young man with black hair showed up at her place looking for you. She told him you were up here and wouldn't be back for another month."

Kira looked up to see Lukas staring at her. "They're not giving up, Kira," he said.

Eva put her arm around Kira. Kira straightened and clasped her hands together. "Well, good for them because I'm not giving up either. Not when they've threatened an innocent child."

Lukas stood by Ruby's front window overlooking the street. A blanket of fresh snow lay over the houses, vehicles, and roadway. The faint lights from the modular homes speared the street edged by parked snowmobiles. A few trucks loomed up the street, but he couldn't see anything moving. He drew a sharp breath. Someone close by had stalked them tonight and taken pictures. A photograph of Sophie! Anger coiled in his stomach like snakes.

He'd been so careful in his survey of the restaurant. There were no new faces. The text messages beneath the photos proved they weren't a harmless teenage prank. The threats were veiled but not directives for her to produce the flash drive—yet. And now a stranger had shown up at Aunt June's in Winnipeg asking for Kira.

He swung away from the window and said, "Have you been seeing anyone in Winnipeg? This guy who turned up at Aunt June's—could he be somebody you dated?"

Kira flushed, but she met his gaze head on. "I'm not dating anybody, down there or anywhere else." She shifted on the couch. "And if I were, Aunt June would know him."

A resounding *boom* shook the building. The front window shattered in its frame, and pictures on the walls tumbled to the floor. Eva pitched forward off the couch as Kira tried to hold onto her. Lukas fell to his side and covered his head with his hands. Sophie shrieked from her bedroom.

Sophie.

An aftershock rocked the building. More glass crashed downstairs. As the sound waves dissipated, he forced himself up and ran down the hallway. Ruby rushed out of her room, putting a hand on each wall to steady herself.

"Is everyone all right?" She clutched a robe around her. "What's happening?"

"I don't know, stay in the living room with Kira. I'm getting Sophie."

His head wobbled from the repercussion of the force of the blast. His feet slid on the floor as he ran into Sophie's room. Her face screwed up in tears, and her screams pierced the air. She held out her arms to him. He grabbed her up with her pink bedspread, throwing it over her head in case they encountered fire.

"Lukas!" Kira yelled, and then coughed and gagged in the living room. He could move faster now. He had Sophie safe in his arms. The living room contained dark grey smoke, but it wasn't rising. It hung heavy in the air. The living room window looked like the ball from a crane had smashed it in. Eva stood by the front door she'd opened.

"You shouldn't have opened the door Eva," he said, gesturing at Kira to grab her afghan, "there's a fire downstairs."

"I don't think so," Eva said, "there's no heat, and I don't hear the roaring sounds of a fire."

"Here, can you take her?" He thrust Sophie at Kira. "I'm going downstairs to see what's going on." He didn't bother tying his shoes. He just shoved his feet into them. "Stay in the bathroom. It's the safest place."

Sophie wailed and reached for him. He ignored her—*oh, my precious heart*—and double-timed it down the rear stairs into the restaurant. Heavy smoke greeted him as soon as he went through the restaurant doors. He covered his mouth and nose to protect himself from inhaling it. Should he go back upstairs and get the others? Or should he call 911 first?

He took a second to check towards the kitchen to see if there was a fire because Eva was right, there was no heat. He held his other hand out in front of him through the smoke, walking over shattered china tableware and glass on the floor. The oak tables and chairs lay strewn like bowling pins.

People climbed inside the shattered front window and over the debris of Christmas decorations, glass, and wood. Voices came to him through the smoke. His eyes burned. Another smell assaulted him. Not smoke, not rubber, but something he couldn't put his finger on. More like an oily garage smell.

"Lukas!" Kira's voice came from behind him.

"Where's Sophie? I gave her to you."

"It's okay, Ruby's got her. She wouldn't stop crying till Ruby held her." Kira coughed, although the worst of the smoke was wafting away now. He gestured her forward and took her hand as they surveyed the damage. His vision blurred as he thought of all the hours he'd spent eating and enjoying life with his friends in this place. Not to mention it was Ruby's livelihood and her family's legacy.

The Café side with its now open-air window would take days to repair. And what chance did they have of getting a new storefront picture window up here this time of year? If the weather held they could fly one up in a week, maybe less. But only if that storm front didn't move in further.

He blew out a breath. "I thought it was an earthquake or tremor, but this is like a bomb went off..."

"It's exactly like a bomb went off." Kira turned in place. "It looks like a news story from the Middle East."

The recognizable RCMP siren sounded down the road. Lukas put both his hands on Kira's shoulders. "I need to see if there are any small fires. Stay here."

"Not a chance," she said. "I'll get the fire extinguisher from the kitchen."

He sighed. Stubborn. "Fine. But it's an industrial-sized extinguisher. Get someone to help you lift it, okay? You shouldn't do it alone with your concussion." He squeezed her shoulder. "I'll check the rest of the dining room."

He grabbed two men who'd climbed in the shattered window and told them what to look for regarding fire sparks. They needed to make sure nothing would ignite. The RCMP snowmobile came to a stop at the edge of the crowd, and a large figure shut it off. The crimson light continued flashing in circles.

The RCMP officer strode towards the building. Tall and massive through his shoulders, the officer held everyone's gaze as he came through the café door.

"Can anyone tell me what happened here?"

"Some kind of explosion," Kira said from behind Lukas. She'd brought the enormous fire extinguisher out with help and rolled it to a stop with a short puff of breath. Another woman stood beside her.

"Is everyone all right?" The officer removed his muskrat hat and leather gloves. "Is anyone unaccounted for?"

Lukas shook his head. "The café was closed for the night. My daughter, my friend, her assistant, the owner, and I were the only ones here in the upstairs apartment."

"The volunteer fire department is on their way, just in case we need them."

"Good because some of the explosive material might still be combustible," Lukas said.

Turning towards the men picking through the rubble, the police officer said, "I'll need you to retrace your steps to the front of the restaurant, please. We can't disturb what could be evidence."

Eva and Ruby picked their way through the debris. Ruby held Sophie on her hip. Wrapped in her pink bedspread, the little girl peered at everyone with her thumb in her mouth.

"Oh, my stars. Why would someone want to destroy my Café?" Ruby asked, her eyes wide. "Who would do such a thing?"

Lukas patted her shoulder. "I'll try to rustle up plywood we can hammer over the window to keep out the cold and any teens who might get funny ideas about looting the place."

Ruby shivered and drew the bedspread tighter around Sophie. "Lukas, what's going on?"

"We're working to find out." He spoke sharper than he intended. "At least the Emporium side is intact. It could've been teens looking for a thrill."

"No," Kira said, her voice trembling. "It's because of me. I'm the reason you're all in danger. I'm so sorry, Ruby."

"Now why would that be, Miss?" the officer asked.

"Someone attacked me, and now they've escalated to this." She motioned with her hand. "This is serious business."

"You must be Kira Summers then?" the officer asked. "I've read over Constable Koper's reports. I flew in this afternoon from Thompson just before the weather took a turn. We'll need to talk." He gestured with his hand to encompass the café. "First, I need to take photographs and see if there's anything left of whatever exploded."

"Sure," Kira said, "I'll be over here whenever you need me."

Lukas took in her pallor and the shadows under her eyes. *Her concussion.*

"Kira, you should be checked out again for your head." He held his index finger up to her. "Watch my finger," he said as he drew a quick square in the air. She tracked it fine till he got to the right side.

"That blast might've done more damage. You should see Dr. Stedman or whoever's on duty at the health centre."

"I need to leave." She turned away and then swung around again to shove the fire extinguisher towards him. "I'm putting you all in danger."

Lukas put a hand on the extinguisher and stopped it from falling over.

"Kira, where're you going now?" he called after her as she ran to the back stairs.

"I'm getting my stuff and clearing out of here."

Lukas strode through the debris on the floor to the staircase. She shuddered, and he pulled her against his chest.

"You're not going anywhere. The safest place is to stay with me."

"No! Look what's happened. Ruby's place is a disaster. This café's been here for forty-five years!" She buried her face into his shirt. "What do they want, Lukas?"

He caressed her hair, smoothing it down her neck as she turned her face sideways and sniffled. It felt right—no, it felt good—to be holding her again. He brought his hand around to her chin and tipped it up so he could see her face.

"Darlin', we will figure it out. Corporal Mackenzie's here now to help." He rubbed his thumb along her cheek, and she leaned into his hand. "Please, stay."

Kira looked into his eyes. The depths of her hazel eyes rimmed with brown made his heart quiver. She was *here* in his arms once more even if he could read uncertainty in her eyes. Her lips parted, and he lowered his head to hers. Was he taking advantage of her emotions? The need to kiss her thudded in his chest.

"Lukas..." His name was a sigh on her lips. She pressed against him, reaching up on her toes to meet his mouth. He kissed her, the endorphins sizzling in his brain. She tasted like cocoa and peppermint. He deepened the kiss, forgetting where they stood, in front of strangers and his daughter.

Kira moved her head to the left, breaking the kiss. She nuzzled her cheek on his as he laced his fingers through the back of her hair, taking a steadying breath. What was he thinking? He wasn't thinking. That much was clear, but nothing would change the fact that she'd responded to him. She'd wanted the kiss as much as he had. His heart ached to kiss her again.

A cough and a throat clearing brought him back to their surroundings. Kira sank back to her feet and put her fingers to her lips.

"Now that we know for sure you're okay over there, maybe I can take some statements?" The corporal's grin split his face in two.

Lukas loosened his arms around Kira. She shook her head, but from what he could tell, she was smiling.

"We'll be right with you, sir," Lukas said. He put his chin on the top of her head for a second, wanting to keep the moment alive. Just a bit longer. If only.

Kira's breathing returned to normal.

What am I doing? It's just the scare—he's trying to reassure me, that's all.

She took a step backwards and disengaged herself from the embrace. The corporal looked to be about forty, his hair silvering just a smidge at the temples. His grey eyes snapped with laughter as he looked at her. She groaned inside. She'd behaved so unprofessionally in front of someone whose help she needed.

"Sorry, I was going upstairs to pack." She touched her fingers to her lips. "Sir, would it be better if I slept in one of those cells at your detachment? I'm afraid it's the only way my friends will be safe."

He looked her over, tapping his notebook against his long parka, as though he were considering it.

"I'm solo right now until we can free up another officer from Thompson or Lynn Lake. I can't be at the detachment 24/7 watching you, however safe you might be in a cell. Besides, we've got suspects to track down, Ms. Summers."

"I'm a danger to my friends." She couldn't keep the tremor out of her voice. "This guy, or whoever it is, is stalking us, attacking me, blowing things up." Anger roared like lava through her veins. So it was true, a person could see red from emotions. Spots blurred her vision, and she was tired of her heart pumping extra beats from fear. It was time to change things.

"Let's take those photos and get samples of the debris and explosive residue, if we can find any." She put her hands on her hips. "I'm a scientist, so can I stand in for one of your forensics people?"

Corporal Mackenzie unzipped his parka and took out his cell phone. "Pictures from this will have to do. Let's start at the front and work our way back, shall we?"

Lukas touched her shoulder. "Are you sure your head's all right?"

"I need to do this." She held his hand and caressed the back of it for a second. "I'll be fine. I'll come and get you if I feel woozy."

He quirked the side of his mouth up as if to say, *yeah, sure you will.*

"This is a crime scene now, right?" he asked the officer.

"Yes, it is, and we can board over that window. But I'm afraid the Café and Emporium is closed till we're finished processing it." Corporal Mackenzie huffed out a breath. "And the forensic ident tech left this afternoon on the same charter plane I came in on. Nothing we can do about it now. Who'd have thought this small town would have crimes like this back to back?"

Lukas turned to Ruby. "It's your turn to come stay at my place. The Great Northern Lodge and the other hotels are fully booked. Can you pack enough stuff for a couple of days?"

"I don't want to put you out, Lukas."

"Nonsense. After everything you've done for me, we'll make it work."

"There're some unused rooms out at the ASRC," Kira said. "Eva, could you take Ruby and Sophie back there for a night or two?"

"Sure can. Should we ask Professor Birchall first?"

"I'm coming out with you, too. The only way everyone will be safe is if I leave town and go back where I belong," she said. "I'm sure he'll understand when we explain it to him."

"I don't feel right being all the way out there when my property's in such a state," Ruby said.

"Kira's right, the safest place right now is the ASRC," Lukas said. "Even if it's just for tonight, take the girls and Sophie out there till Corporal Mackenzie assesses the crime scene."

Kira's emotions rippled along her last nerve. She struggled to focus. "Well, I'm going to stay for now so I can help collect evidence for the corporal. I'll see you out there when we're done."

"Just for a night or two, then," Ruby said. She rubbed Sophie's shoulders. "C'mon, little one, we're going on another adventure." She turned to Kira and Eva. "I'll be back with a few things. Don't anyone leave without me."

Kira gave her a tired smile. There'd be hours of work before she could leave. Everyone's breath plumed in the frigid air. Lukas appeared at her side with her coat. Suddenly shy, she zipped up her parka and nodded at him before heading to the front of the café.

She'd let Lukas kiss her. Not just kiss her, she'd enjoyed it. The door to their past had opened a crack, letting in fresh air to sweep away old hurt. And that could be her downfall.

CHAPTER 10

A week later, the sky poured bright sunshine down over the bay and tundra. Kira drank in the fresh cold air outside Lukas's house. Dr. Stedman still insisted she limit her screen time, but at least her hands had healed enough that she only needed to put some light cream on at bedtime. No more bandages. Her headache persisted, but she could manage without pain pills now.

Kira watched Lukas wrangle Timber into his harness at the head of the sled team. The other dogs barked and jumped in anticipation of the run ahead. Jonah held on to the back of the tandem sleds while the new clients figured out who wanted to be in what order. There was room for all eight of them between the two sleds harnessed together.

Kira stopped Sophie from eating snow, even though it was pristine and white. Since the bombing at the café, Kira was hyper-aware of her surroundings.

This must be what soldiers with PTSD feel like. The constant revving in her chest that wouldn't go away, or the feeling she was being watched, even when she stood alone at Lukas's kitchen door, looking across the flat terrain. She hated these violent emotions surging through her. She wanted peace in her life again, but it would take catching whoever was after her and those she loved.

Those she loved.

Where had that come from? She knelt beside Sophie as the little girl scooped up more snow and threw it in the air, trying to catch it on her tongue again. This beautiful child had entered a space in her heart she hadn't known existed. She'd always thought of having children someday. That *someday*, though, was before Derek Straughn. Who wanted to raise a child in a world containing that kind of evil? But Sophie had broken through that rock-solid wall in her heart with her purity, her innocence, and her enjoyment of the simple things in her world. It was easy to see things from Sophie's perspective because she was incapable of hate or negativity, thanks to what others saw as her disability. And Lukas's parenting had given her a secure and emotionally stable life.

Those she loved.

Lukas. He was petting each dog on the head as he walked down the harness line. She still loved him. Why was that a shock to her system? He'd stood fast when she needed him, protected her, given her shelter and wise counsel.

The clients seemed innocuous enough. Could one of them be the stalker? She shivered from her thoughts, not the cold. Lukas told her he'd seen no strangers in the restaurant the night those photos were taken. Maybe there was something suspicious about Mr. and Mrs. Eldridge. They were repeat customers on their fourth trip to see the bears and wildlife. Lukas vouched for them and didn't consider them suspects, but what new delights did they expect to see on a fourth trip? There was a honeymooning couple on their first trip to Churchill. Mr. Cranston gestured his wife forward, but she stood with her boots planted firmly in the snow. Her arms were crossed, and she pulled away from his hand while he tried to convince her to get on the sled. No, she wasn't going to enjoy sitting behind eight dogs at ground level.

The last couple had two young children. Lukas hadn't introduced them to her, but they looked like a typical family traveling with a boy and girl about ten and twelve. The children were jumping up and down and arguing over who would sit at the front of the sled. Lukas stooped down to their level and had them pick one of his fisted gloves to find an object. The boy whooped and hollered after he picked the glove holding a smooth stone. He ran to the front of the sled and sat down even though his mother tried to caution him not to scare the dogs.

"No worries, Mrs. Lee. These dogs don't scare easily. About the only thing they're scared of is a polar bear, and we're not going anywhere near that area this morning." Lukas's smile was infectious.

"Mrs. Cranston, will you please sit behind the Lees?" He gestured with his left arm towards the sled. Jonah was having a hard time holding the sled in place as the dogs panted and bucked, eager to be on their way. The woman sullenly took a seat behind Mrs. Lee. Her husband perched behind her and put his legs to the outside of her thighs, tightening his grip.

Last on were the Eldredges. Lukas took the helm from Jonah and set his boots on the back of the sled. Sophie tugged to get loose, holding out her arms for him, but Kira held her fast.

"We're not going with Daddy this time, bug." She hefted Sophie up on her hip and helped her wave goodbye.

"Actually, we can go with the second sled if you'd like to try it out," Jonah offered.

"I've only seen Lukas's dogs around. There's other dogs here?"

"They're my dogs. I brought them over when Lukas asked me to stay and watch his place last week." Jonah nodded towards the barn. "I can harness them up in two minutes."

"Sure," she said. "I've never been dog sledding. Is it safe enough for Sophie?"

"We'll put her snowmobile helmet on her in case there's a tumble. But my dogs are older than Lukas's and not as rambunctious." He smiled. "I don't race them anymore."

He gave Lukas a sign, whirling his right index finger in the air; Lukas nodded and waved.

"Timber, ho! Team, ho!"

The dogs jerked ahead, the sled pulling with resistance against the snow and gliding forward. The clients' sleds moved out down to the road in front of Lukas's property, with the dogs yipping as they ran.

"That looks like so much fun!" Kira said. "Can we follow them?"

"Just give me a sec." Jonah headed over to the barn.

She hadn't been out there since she'd found the polar bear tracks. She stood in the sunlight glittering across the snow. The stunted trees and buildings stood out in relief against the azure-blue canopy of sky. Sophie wanted down so Kira set her on her bottom in the snow. Snow up here was dry—not wet snowman snow like in the south. It carried large ice crystals that glittered against Kira's gloves. She was alone for the first time since this ordeal started. Alone in a clear landscape where she could see to the horizon. Sophie chattered away at her boots, making patterns in the snow with her mitts.

So why did she sense a menacing presence nearby?

Kira would've rather been on Lukas's dog sled, but the morning run was everything she'd imagined it would be. The brilliant sunshine and whooshing sound of the sled against the snow delighted Sophie, and Kira held the toddler tight against her chest so they didn't roll off traveling around corners. The anxiety and fear Kira carried on her shoulders lifted for the first time since coming back home. She readjusted Sophie's scarf over her little nose and mouth as they slowed down going around another corner.

Coming back home. There were those intrusive thoughts again. As far as she was concerned, nowhere had been home in the past five years. She'd always thought of herself as a lab rat, just putting up with the inconvenience of outdoor experiments and studies. But out here, riding on the flat terrain rolling out to the never-ending horizon of the sky, the freedom of being one with the wilderness filled her with a sense of awe. A sense of God's majesty. She didn't want the trail ride to end.

Ruby was watching for them at the door of Lukas's house when they zoomed into the yard. Jonah's dogs continued half-running in a circle before they came to a stop. With tongues lolling and eyes bright, they dropped down on the snow in their traces. Sophie clapped her hands and reached forward.

"Me, me, me!" she said as she flopped forward on the sled. Her loose hips and limbs allowed her to touch her boot tips.

"No, honey, we need to get off the sled before you can see the dogs." Kira let Ruby lift Sophie off her lap. For the first time, she felt a sense of loss when Sophie left her arms, and she almost said, "Bring her back," but Jonah already had his hand out to help her stand.

"Can she pet them?" Kira asked, gesturing to the panting dogs.

"Sure," Jonah said. He took Sophie by the hand and led her to the first dog, hunkering down beside her while she patted the husky on the head.

"She sure loves animals," Ruby observed. "I keep teasing Lukas that he's going to have to figure out how to keep a pony up here soon."

Kira brushed the fresh snow off her snow pants. "It was lovely. What a rush! Very different than snowmobiling."

"Better for the environment, too," Ruby said. "Are you staying for lunch?"

"No, we're meeting Lukas and his clients at the railway station restaurant and then heading out to the Wildlife Management Area from there."

A shadow touched Ruby's face. "I'm sorry I couldn't fulfill my part of the contract, but I have no kitchen to serve anything out of at the moment."

Kira patted her on the shoulder. "Lukas understands. We should hear back in a couple of weeks about those samples of explosive residue from the cafe." She pulled out snowmobile keys. "Lukas said Jonah and I could take his snowmobiles back into town. The snow's finally deep enough."

Jonah brought Sophie up the steps to the front deck. "Here's our beautiful Soph-Soph." He handed her off to Ruby. "Ready to go?" he asked Kira.

"It's been awhile since I've driven one, but it's like riding a bike, right?" She tugged on her long snowmobile mitts and picked up a helmet from the full box of gear on the deck. "Hot pink! You won't lose me with this on!"

She tucked in her hair around the sides of the helmet and settled it on her head. The peripheral vision was good, and she was eager to get into town for lunch and the afternoon tour. Jonah followed her across the yard to the two parked snowmobiles.

"Lukas keeps these for emergencies," he said. "He promised they'd be gassed up."

Kira settled onto her seat and turned the key in the ignition. The snowmobile rumbled underneath her. Then she looked both ways before throttling forwards. They raised their hands to wave at Ruby and Sophie as they left the yard and headed straight across the tundra towards town. Again, Kira felt a twinge at leaving the little girl behind. She was getting attached. And that was something Lukas probably wouldn't appreciate, given their current circumstances.

What circumstances are those? Lukas didn't owe her anything, and he was giving her a lot. She needed to protect her heart, or she'd get it broken. She'd thrown a marriage proposal back in his face. He had no reason to trust her now.

Within twenty minutes, they pulled up outside the historical railway station. The small restaurant inside served only breakfast and lunch. They'd been happy to accommodate Lukas's tour group after the explosion at Ruby's Café.

The group filled the restaurant with high-pitched chatter. Kira grabbed a cold meat sandwich from the buffet table and headed over to sit with Lukas.

"How's Sophie?" were the first words out of his mouth.

"She loved Jonah's dogs. You've got a real animal lover on your hands." Her shoulder brushed his, sending a flash of heat up her body as she shifted to get comfortable in her seat. "But she's happy to be at home with Ruby." That warmth, that thrill, she had to stop thinking about it. "You're not worried about that bear still, are you?"

Lukas shrugged. "Sarah Thorvald seems to think it's the same one that attacked Ben, and if so, it's securely locked up at the Polar Bear Jail."

He polished off the remainder of his sandwich and wiped his hands on a napkin. "I talked to Ben on the phone. He's going to be in for about five days because of his head trauma. His shoulder may need another surgery in Winnipeg, but they're going to wait and see how it heals."

"That's horrible! That bear should be euthanized. Even if they take it 200 miles north, we can't be sure it won't swing back down around here again. It's a hard decision."

Kira paused. "On the other hand, I'm not so sure—the paw prints were much deeper from the bear that attacked Ben. Two bears might have been out there."

Lukas rubbed his beard scruff. "Maybe I should call Ruby again."

Kira put her hand on his forearm. "She knows to keep Sophie indoors. She'll phone us if she spots a bear or anything else out of place."

He sighed. "I know you're right. I can't help worrying."

Kira squeezed his arm. "You're a wonderful father, so that goes without saying."

He leaned in towards her. Kira felt his energy roll over her. Breathless, she waited to see if he would keep coming closer. He stopped a hairsbreadth from her temple, and his lips brushed her hair in the lightest of kisses.

"Thanks. That means a lot coming from you."

Kira felt her heart stop. Or was it just the moment frozen in her mind? Since their kiss at the bottom of Ruby's stairs, she'd thought of little else. Memories of kisses stolen at youth group, in parking lots, at baseball games. She wanted another kiss, a kiss to bring back every feeling they'd ever had for each other. A kiss to end their separation and make her part of his life.

Whoa. This was getting out of hand. She wasn't a real part of his life; he was doing this for Michael's sake. She'd brought danger into his and Sophie's carefully prescribed routine. Nothing could hurt that precious little girl. Nothing. She would disappear again before that happened.

Lukas briefly rested his forehead against her temple and then straightened. Standing up, he said, "We need to get rolling, people, if we're going to see the best of the wildlife out there. Please hit the washrooms and grab your cameras and cold weather gear. We'll be leaving in ten minutes."

Everyones' voices rose over and flowed around each other. The guests geared up with backpacks and extra snacks and headed out to Lukas's Arctic Rover for the wildlife tour.

The thirty-five-foot-long Arctic Rover was a renovated school bus Lukas had painted navy blue. He'd built a metal deck off the back door so people could be outside and observe the animals through the deck's high plexiglass walls. Custom-made tank treads fit around its wheels so as not to affect the fragile environment of the tundra. Lukas owned two rovers, although other tour companies owned more. He'd installed an indoor bathroom and broad, sideways cushioned seats down each side. Today was sunny enough that the clients vied for space at the side windows, trying to get the best photograph of the family of silver Arctic foxes trotting alongside them.

As Lukas drove farther into the Wildlife Management Area, he gave his usual lecture, relating facts about the birds, animals, and subarctic ecological system while keeping the tourists engaged in playing "Who can spot the sleeping polar bears?" It was a game the tourists liked to play. Kira sat down on the opposite side of the rover and relaxed while she watched the group's excitement for this frozen, stark, beautiful land she loved so much.

Lukas talked comfortably with his clients. His big, square hands turned and settled the steering wheel of the rover when they rolled up and down on the pathway. The tension he'd carried in his shoulders was gone. While she knew he was still worried about Ben, being in the outdoors with these strangers relaxed him.

He was no longer the willful, reckless youth she'd fallen in love with back in high school. He showed no trace of arrogance, just a deep self-confidence that spoke of knowing who he was—a father and a grown man. She admired his deep security and sense of self and wondered when, if ever, she'd feel that herself.

He had been crazy in love with her. Ruby had said it, and deep down, Kira knew it was true. Unwelcome tears pricked the backs of her eyes as she stared at the white terrain outside the window. She deserved true love, didn't she? She wiped her cheeks with her fingertips. Well, welcome to the pity party! It wasn't enough that her heart was more bitter than a Granny apple. Now she felt sorry for herself as well.

She'd let that college attack define her life.

Kira sat up straight as the realization hit her. It was true... everything she'd run away from went back to *that night*. But she wasn't that girl anymore. She'd made some bad choices, beginning with falling for Derek's threats and ending with not trusting Lukas with the truth. She'd run instead of facing what had happened to her, instead of letting others help her. And fear and bitterness had ruled her life.

Kira covered her mouth with her hand as the tears came fast and furious. She turned her face towards the window to hide her tears and huddled against the bus wall.

Oh, God, I'm so sorry. I left You, too! I left everyone and everything You had provided for me, and I let Derek and his unspeakable evil win the day.

She fought to keep herself under control. Being in control had been her touchstone for so long.

God, please help me find the right way to tell Lukas what I did and ask his forgiveness. Even if it means he rejects me, even if I lose him forever.

Blowing her nose and wiping her eyes gave her a measure of comfort. Her heart lightened. Lukas deserved to know the truth. He had asked her to marry him. He had loved her once. Even if they had no future together, he deserved to know the truth.

Kira let her body rock back and forth, going with the movement of the rover. It was soothing, and she was glad her concussion headache had dulled to a manageable level. She was starting to feel human again. She stuffed her tissue in her pocket and popped a peppermint in her mouth.

Lukas brought the rover to a stop near an inukshuk about two feet high. It wasn't large and symmetrical like the one back on the main beach. That one had stood sentinel for many years. This was a small pile of rocks someone had made into as human a figure as they could, given the flat rocks thereabout. Lukas turned in his driver's seat.

"The word *inukshuk* is the Inuit's word for 'that which acts in capacity of a human.' Hunters leave them on the tundra to point out the way they've come or where they're going. It's an ancient communication system." He waited for the boy to settle back onto his seat and be quiet. "Someone's made this inukshuk for a reason, but I don't know what it might be. I've never seen it here before."

Kira saw a flash of something moving out the window. She moved to the left side of the rover and put her hands around her eyes against the window to block out the sun's glare. It was a feathered wing, and the breeze was ruffling the feathers of whatever bird was lying there. It wasn't unusual to see dead birds or animals—but something about the color of these feathers wasn't right.

"I'm sorry to interrupt," she said as she moved towards the front of the rover, "but I need to step outside and check on something."

Lukas raised his left eyebrow. "You know we don't leave the rover for any reason. We're close to bear territory now."

"I want to check something—I promise I'll be quick."

Sighing, he pulled on the lever to open the door. "Kira, thirty seconds, that's it."

She went down the steps and hopped down to the ground. With her head on a swivel looking from right to left for bears, she headed over to the pile of feathers fluttering in the wind and skidded to a stop. While the tundra appeared to be flat, it hid small mounds, crevices, dips, and rolling rock formations. Polar bears were especially fond of sleeping curled up against the rocks.

The dead gull lay coated in a slimy, yellow substance she'd never seen before. It looked fresh. In her heart, she had a sinking feeling she knew what it meant. If only she had her field supply kit with her. Instead, Kira pulled an empty sandwich bag from her parka pocket and used a stick to scrape some of the viscous material into the little plastic bag. She squatted down and piled rocks high beside the bird so she could come back and find it again.

Lukas came up behind her. "We need to go. You shouldn't be out here. It's dangerous. You know that."

She shoved herself to her feet, brushing off her snow pants. "Lukas," she breathed, "look at this." She pointed towards the rocks at her feet.

Bright orangey-yellow water spiraled in frozen trails across the stones and around the dead bird. As she stepped forward to go over the dead gull, she slipped on a frozen patch of it. She kept her balance by windmilling her arms. Farther down the rocky beach, she could see other coloured frozen areas. And was that a dead fox or other small mammal beside more rocks?

This was a southern section of the Wildlife Management Area Kira hadn't been in for a while. And that vivid orange frozen along the gravelly rock stretched at least an eighth of a mile up the shore. Not a huge area but significant if it was what she was afraid of. At least it hadn't reached the actual Bay waters but stayed on land.

"I've gotta get pictures of this," she said, whipping out her phone. "Professor Birchall needs to see this right away."

She snapped photographs, jumping from one rocky area to another, heading over to the big lump she saw beside a pile of rocks. Taking a breath, she uploaded the pictures in a text to her boss. Her heart pounded her sternum like a sledgehammer.

"Lukas! Something's moving down here," she yelled before she slid into the coloured rocks on her knees. Now she could hear the faint catlike sounds of a baby. A baby what? She stood and slipped and slid over to the pile of rocks and discovered they weren't rocks at all. Beside the dirty and yellowy-orange streaked polar bear mother was a bear cub, whimpering its distress. The mother lay inert, no breaths raising her sides at all. Kira's heart beat triple time. Could she trust it was already dead? And what had killed it—the mystery water or a hunter? She slid off her parka, all the while making cooing sounds to the cub. It appeared to be about seven months old from this year's birthing but on the small side, maybe forty-five or fifty pounds.

Lukas appeared at her side. "Kira! We can't... what are you doing?"

"Saving it," she said before she resettled her parka on the ground and slid it towards the bear cub. "Are you going to help me or not?"

Lukas scanned the immediate area for other bears. This looked like it had been the entrance to a maternal den, but it didn't mean other bears weren't nearby. He held the shotgun with cracker shells loosely in his right hand as he tried to steady Kira with his left.

"I can't leave the clients, Kira. We need to come back with proper help. This is a job for the natural resource officers, not us."

"Just give me a minute, and I'll have it scooped up here."

She crouched on her heels and duck-walked forwards, sliding her parka in front of her. The mother's body still lay motionless. She must be dead. The fur on the bear cub's paws stuck out in spikes with the orange gunk. Taking a deep breath, Kira reached forward and grasped the cub by its neck, pulling it onto her parka and dragging them back to her.

"Kira!" His pulse roared in his ears. He'd never seen anything like this orange water, but it seemed confined to this short stretch of shoreline. He had to contact the natural resource's office and Corporal Mackenzie as soon as they got back to the Arctic Rover. "We've got to go, now."

He pulled on Kira's upper arm to help her stand as she grasped the squirming bear cub inside her parka. They both wavered on their feet to get their balance.

"It's okay, Lukas, it's alive at least. We need to..."

The blast of firecrackers went off around them. Not firecrackers, bullets. Just as Lukas registered the sound, pieces of rocks burst upwards around them. Bullets shot up the ground close to them. He swung around, firing off a cracker shell, not that it would do anything besides give their attackers a sound wave boom. He grabbed Kira by the arm again and dragged her towards the rover.

Kira ran with her head down, the parka against her chest. More bullets cracked off the rocks. Lukas hauled her towards the stairs of the rover just as a bullet hit his left shoulder. The impact whirled him around and he fell backwards onto the stairs, shooting another cracker shell back towards the onslaught of bullets.

Two people on a snowmobile drove in a wide circle around his Arctic Rover. The person riding on the back of it fired a high-powered rifle at his vehicle. He couldn't tell who they were; their helmets and full snowmobile suits gave them anonymity.

Jonah grabbed him under the right shoulder and helped him scramble up the stairs. They pulled the rover door shut from the inside.

"Get away from the windows," Lukas yelled.

The clients screamed. The Lees children were burrowed beneath the seats. Kira handed off the bundle with the bear cub to Mrs. Cranston, who fell backwards onto the far seat as it tried to wriggle free.

"I need my other rifle!" Lukas shook off Jonah and pointed to the overhead bin.

"Forget that..." Kira pumped a shell into his shotgun and opened the rover's back door to the outside observation deck. When had she had time to grab it? Holding it at shoulder height, she fired a shell at the snowmobile, towards the roadway. Its loud crack echoed across the wide-open space. The clients shrieked louder, hands over their ears, flat on the floor of the rover.

Another bullet smashed through the plexiglass of the outside back deck from the road side, and Lukas could hear Kira yelling.

Waves of nausea hit him, and he couldn't get off the floor. Kira appeared, looming over him.

"They're getting away. Lukas, sweetheart, look at me."

He tried to focus on her face, but the edges of his vision blurred.

"We have to call Corporal Mackenzie."

"Here's my phone," Mr. Cranston said, his hand coming out from underneath a seat.

"Lukas, you're bleeding." Kira's face faded.

He was bleeding? He should've done a better job protecting her.

"Lukas?" She sounded far away.

The ceiling of the rover swirled downwards.

CHAPTER 11

A hot poker speared Lukas's left shoulder to the floor. His left arm rippled with fire. Someone sat on his chest and alternately squeezed and pulled on his arm. He struggled to open his eyes, and when he did all he could see was the metal roof of his bus. Shouting, crying, and the boy's wails flowed over him.

"You're lucky," Jonah said. "I think it's only a flesh wound, but we need to get your shoulder checked out at the health centre. Don't move or the bleeding will start again."

Lukas squeezed his eyes shut. *Oh Lord, this is agony!* He'd done a great job protecting Kira. If he kept his eyes shut and concentrated, he could hear her voice above the hubbub. Her words cracked like the gunfire that just hit them.

"They're gone. There's no way we could catch them; they were on a snowmobile." He could see Kira looking out the rover's window towards town while holding the phone against her ear. "There were two, on a black snowmobile, I couldn't see what type it was... It looked like a high-powered scope rifle—but I could be wrong." She paused. "Yes, they shot Lukas in the shoulder." Another pause. "Well, I hope Jonah knows how to drive this thing because I sure don't."

"I can drive; I'll be fine," Lukas said.

"No way, old man," Jonah said. "We're going to sit you up and lay you on one of the seats. Do you think you can get up?"

"Of course I can," Lukas said. He inhaled and gritted his teeth. His left arm hung useless. With his right forearm, he grasped Jonah's left arm and allowed himself to be pulled to a sitting position.

"Okay, just sit there for a second till we know you're okay."

"Yes, I'll tell him. Thank you, corporal." Kira handed back the phone and came to the front of the bus to crouch down beside him. He could see the worry and fear in her eyes and felt like cursing under his breath. Whoever those guys were, he wanted to hunt them down and... He closed his eyes again. He struggled to push those thoughts out of his mind. Anger gnawed in his stomach making him nauseous again. The attackers roared up on their snowmobile as cool as you please and shot at them. At Kira! His clients! Feeling murderous rage was a human reaction, but he breathed a prayer for forgiveness.

Well, now they'd seen the crazy orange water trickling on the shoreline, he had a good idea what those emails were about and why Michael had wanted to talk to him. Webster Technologies had dumped illegal hazardous waste. Whether it was an accident or on purpose remained to be seen.

"I'm okay, darlin'. Honest, I'm going to be okay. Just help me get up," Lukas said. Jonah put his hands under Lukas's right shoulder, while Kira stood and guided them over to the now vacant bench seat. She put a blanket from the side storage unit under his head and helped him lie back down.

"Don't move, you'll start bleeding again. I called 911, and they'll be ready for us at the health centre." Kira covered him with another blanket, then straightened and held on to the upright pole beside the seat. The clients were getting up from the floor. Some sat on the seats, and some huddled together in the center of the rover not knowing what to do with themselves.

"Is everyone okay? Is anyone else hurt?" Kira looked over the group. "Anyone?"

The kids still hiccupped a couple of times. "It's okay, guys," she told them. "It's okay to be scared, but the bad guys are gone now." She looked at the parents. "The RCMP will be on the lookout for that snowmobile going back into town. They know what's happened, and it's not like those guys can get very far in such a small town."

"A snowmobile can disappear into any garage," Mr. Eldridge said. "And how many RCMP officers are there in town?"

"Yeah," Mr. Cranston said, "I heard there was only one guy left since the polar bear got the regular cop." His wife shushed him.

Kira turned to Jonah. "So, do you know how to drive this thing?"

Jonah shrugged. "I can try it. I drove a school bus one year, and it looks like the gears are similar."

Lukas groaned from where he lay on the seat. Fire shot up his arm, and he couldn't move it. He clenched his teeth to stop himself from throwing up. Waves of nausea and freezing cold shot upwards through him.

"Hang in there, buddy. I'll try not to wreck your super-vehicle." Jonah sat behind the steering wheel. He looked in the rearview mirror at the clients. "I suggest you all sit down and get settled. This thing only goes twenty-five kilometers an hour, so we're not going to catch up to those idiots. Don't worry, we won't cross paths with them."

"But what if they come back to get us?" the Lees' boy asked, his eyes wide and fearful.

"Why were they shooting at us, anyway?" his dad asked. "That bear cub? Were you allowed to take it?"

Kira swayed in rhythm to the rover rolling over the terrain as she held onto the seat where Lukas lay. "The bear cub is mine, and you don't need to be concerned," she said. She smiled at the son. "Anyway, they're gone now, and I don't think they'll be coming back. Okay?"

The fiery pain spread across his chest and down to his fingertips. Lukas moaned. If this was a through and through, he'd hate to know what a bullet in the bone felt like. Lukas ground his teeth against a slight roll of the rover as it sent more blistering pain through his shoulder and arm.

Yeah, tough guy. Show her you can take the pain. What's a little bullet between friends?

It took twenty-five minutes to get back into town. As Jonah brought the rover to a standstill at the door of the health centre, two nurses brought out a gurney. Kira helped him sit up and then put his good arm over her shoulder and hoisted him to his feet. Everyone stood back so Lukas and Kira could get down the rover steps. She and Jonah helped him sit on the gurney before he swung his legs up. The nurses expertly lifted the gurney back up to its proper height and wheeled him through the emergency room doors.

"I feel like I should move in here," Lukas said. He bit his lip to keep from moaning out loud.

Jonah raised an eyebrow at Kira. She shrugged. "I just got out of here a week ago myself. Lukas stayed with me 'round the clock."

Dr. Stedman appeared with a younger man in surgical scrubs beside him. He looked shocked. "What is it with you two? You're not the usual frequent flyers we get in here." He checked Lukas's pupils with his penlight. "How did this happen?"

Before Lukas could answer, Jonah jumped in. "We were out on his wildlife tour, and Lukas and Kira were trying to rescue a bear cub. And before we knew it, a couple guys on a snowmobile wheeled up and shot at them." He rubbed the beard scruff on his chin. "Lucky for her and Lukas, they weren't great shots. He's winged in the shoulder, but it could've been a lot worse."

Dr. Stedman checked the field dressing while Jonah gave his report. "This is great work. Let's get him into exam room three, and we'll go from there." He looked up at Kira. "Are you sure they weren't natural resource's officers warning you off the bear territory?"

Kira shook her head. "No way. They weren't in uniform, and those weren't warning shots. They fired right at us." She hugged herself across her chest. "And we weren't in bear territory proper, anyway."

"Well, if you want to stay in the waiting room, I'll let you know whether he needs surgery."

Lukas reached for Kira's hand. She leaned across the gurney and whispered in his ear, "I'll be right here waiting for you, all right? Stay strong! You've got this!"

He weakly quirked up the left side of his mouth. Dr. Stedman nodded at the nurse, and they rolled Lukas's gurney down the hallway, rattling and shaking his shoulder till he wanted to scream.

Kira rubbed her forehead, her hyped-up adrenaline rushing out of her system all at once. Exhaustion rooted her boots to the floor. Jonah put his hand on her shoulder.

"Can I get you a coffee or anything?"

"No, thanks, I don't think my heart could take it right now." She couldn't help it, she trembled at the knees. "This is crazy!" she said, "I don't know what to do. How are we supposed to find these guys? There's only one cop in town. We can't expect him to do everything."

"Let's go sit you down in the waiting room," Jonah said. "Why don't you stay here, and I'll drive the clients back to the Great Northern Lodge? They can all get a break and wait for supper."

She sank down on the waiting room couch, rubbing her arms from the cold. "Oh, Jonah, that would be such a relief. I know Lukas would appreciate it, and I'll tell him everything's under control whenever I get to see him."

"Are you sure you'll be okay here alone?" Jonah asked. "Do you want me to call Corporal Mackenzie and have him come over?"

"No, thank you. When I called him from the rover he said he would patrol the outskirts of town and call in the two natural resource's officers to help him, to see if they could spot that snowmobile." She breathed a heavy sigh. "The problem is, I don't know what type of snowmobile it was to identify it." She shook her head. "It was black. The rifle"—she threw her hands out to the sides—"took up all my vision." She put her head in her hands and leaned forward, resting her elbows on her knees.

Jonah shifted on his feet beside her. "You saw more than I did. And you kept your cool, bringing that bear cub back. Speaking of which, I guess I should take it to the Polar Bear Jail, right?"

She gasped, her hand over her mouth. "All I was thinking about was Lukas. Yes, I can call Sarah over at Natural Resources." She dug around in her pants pocket and pulled out her phone. "I'll call her right now and let her know. She can get a cage ready and come into town to pick him up."

"All right then, but you need to keep it somewhere till then. Are you sure you'll be okay here by yourself?" He leaned his shoulder against the wall, but she noticed his eyes followed the nurses and orderlies up and down the hallway.

"Well," she sighed, "I guess I'll have to be. I have no choice." She tapped her phone against her chin. "I know Lukas would want you to look after his clients."

Jonah took one last look around the area and nodded. "I'll keep the cub in the rover till Sarah gets here. Then I'll take the folks over to the lodge. The corporal might need statements from them, too." He strode through the ER doorway, leaving a swirl of frigid air in his wake.

She wasn't about to admit how cold she was; the cub needed her parka more than she did. He also needed a veterinarian checkup, some fluids, and a decontamination bath. She prayed the natural resources officers could deal with whatever substances were on the cub and he'd survive.

Her first call to Sarah went unanswered, so she left an urgent voice-mail message for her to return the call. Then, she left Eva a message to call her back as well.

Pacing the twenty steps back and forth in the waiting area helped. *Okay God, you have my attention. First Michael, then Ben, now Lukas. Am I just a disaster magnet for the men in my life, or is this a spiritual attack? What am I supposed to do? What are You trying to show me?*

The piano riff ring tone on her phone startled her.

"Hello?"

"Kira, what's this about discoloured water out in the Wildlife Management Area and a bear cub?"

123

"Professor Birchall... great! You got my photos."

"Why isn't Natural Resources dealing with it? You're behind enough already on all your DNA experiments."

Kira paused. "They're picking the bear cub up from us here at the hospital. And I knew you'd want to see those photos right away... there's a dead mother polar bear out there and we need to work with Natural Resources to figure out what kind of hazardous waste has killed it."

"Did you show those photos to anyone else?"

"No. Well, Lukas was standing right there beside me. He saw the frozen orange muck. The tourists on the bus saw it. I don't know how we'll clean it up, but we have to report it to the federal government. Who cares if anyone else saw the pictures?"

"And how many tourists did Lukas have on this little tour today?" Birchall asked.

"Eight. It's the last tour of the season."

"How badly is Lukas injured?" Birchall asked.

She paused. Something about his tone of voice didn't sit well with her. Exhaustion swept over her, and she just wanted to get back to Lukas. "Someone shot him. In the shoulder. Just like someone set a fire in my room and attacked me." She took another deep breath. "I know you're all about the bottom line, but could you show some compassion for what everyone's going through right now? If people who work for you aren't safe out at the ASRC, then our numbers are going to drop off, and that means grant money will, too. So it seems to me your bottom line is tied to the security and safety of your scientists. People like me."

"Are you back in the hospital?"

"No, I just said, Lukas was shot."

"Fine. Let me know when you're ready to come back to work."

She drew in the deepest breath she could hold and counted to eight. "Sir, I will let you know when I know." She hung up.

She couldn't contain herself, so she continued to pace in the small waiting room. Dr. Stedman appeared in the door. "You can come and see him now. It was a through and through. He has to stay put for a bit. I've stitched him up and given him some painkillers."

"Oh, thank goodness," she stammered. She wavered on her feet. "Thank you so much."

Dr. Stedman smiled. "And how are you doing? I hope you've been following concussion protocol and staying away from computer screens, TVs, and reading?"

She laughed. "Oh yes, Lukas has been very firm with me. He hasn't let me get away with anything." She pocketed her phone. "So, I can see him now?"

Dr. Stedman motioned her towards the hallway. "He's irritable and barking out orders, but he's all yours."

They headed down between the curtained alcoves to the one displaying number three overhead. Lukas was trying to swing his legs over the side of the gurney. "Hey, buddy, you need to lie down a bit longer," Dr. Stedman said. "That painkiller I gave you won't wear off for another four hours."

"You mean I'm going to be useless for that long?" Lukas's eyes were heavy-lidded, and fine lines of pain crinkled in their corners. "Some guys tried to kill Kira in broad daylight right in front of me. It was only by the grace of God they shot me and not her. I will not lie around while they're still out there."

Dr. Stedman put his hands on his hips. "We have security guards here. You think there's any chance they'd track you guys back here?"

"Never occurred to me," Kira said. "I don't know if they realize Lukas was hit." Her throat tightened. Her tongue stuck to the roof of her mouth. "Lukas, should I call the corporal again?"

Lukas scowled as he held on to his bandaged left shoulder and leaned back again on the gurney. He straightened out his legs and groaned, his face screwed up in pain. "These guards aren't armed, are they?"

"No, they have flashlights and walkie-talkies. I guess they could whack someone with them, but that's about it." Dr. Stedman shrugged. "You'll need physical therapy on that shoulder in about a month. The stitches come out in ten days. But you were lucky it only went through the outer muscle."

"Doc, I don't mean to be rude, but I'm more concerned about being sitting ducks for anyone who can walk in and shoot at us again." Lukas ground his teeth. "Are you sure you gave me something for this pain? Because it hasn't kicked in yet."

"That was a morphine shot. In another minute or two, you'll be seeing pink elephants." Dr. Stedman turned to Kira. "Now, you said you've called the police?"

"Yes, and I'm going to call again for an update." Kira pulled out her phone.

"Outside, please." Dr. Stedman pointed towards the sign prohibiting cell phone use. Kira glanced at Lukas, who'd given in to his pain shot and was losing consciousness. She pulled the blanket up on his chest and tucked it in the sides of his gurney. She hated to leave him for even a second, but getting in touch with Corporal Mackenzie was more important.

"I'll be right back," she whispered. She leaned over and brushed a kiss against his temple. Her lips felt his pulse beating under his skin. *Thank you, Lord, for keeping him alive. Keep us safe!*

She turned and drew the curtains around his gurney before heading out to the ER.

Once in the waiting room, Kira hit speed dial on her phone again for Corporal Mackenzie. It took less than a minute to confirm he was already on his way. Before she could shove her phone back into her pants pocket, the ER doors whooshed open and shut, the cold air swirling in again, raising goose bumps on her arms. Sarah strode in, bundled up in full Arctic gear. She dragged a metal trailer carrying a small travel cage for the bear cub. Sarah looked Kira up and down, her gaze taking in her obvious fatigue and the dirt on her face and clothing. She pulled her gloves off and unzipped her parka, saying, "There's a blizzard coming in from the west. It's looking serious, and the roads will be closed."

"I know. I spoke to Corporal Mackenzie on the phone. The RCMP put it out on social media. Everyone is to stay indoors. There's no reason for anyone to be outside for the next twenty-four hours."

"How's Lukas doing?" Sarah asked. "I heard on the cop channel—did they get the guys who shot him?"

"No, they haven't," Kira said. "Thanks for coming so fast. He needs to be bathed right away, and I want samples of his tainted fur snipped and tested for the chemical makeup because this looks like it could be hazardous waste—possibly mining waste."

Sarah raised an eyebrow at her. "Wow. Okay, where is the little guy?"

"He's actually a medium guy. He's outside in Lukas's Arctic Rover." Kira strode to the outer ER doors, pushing through the frigid air as the doors whooshed open. She waved forwards at Jonah in the driver's seat and nodded "yes" when he held up the swaddled bear cub.

Jonah came down the Rover stairs, holding the cub like a football under his left arm, still wrapped in Kira's parka. It looked like an adorable, small dog, about fifty pounds of cuteness, if you didn't mind the frozen, orange spikes mixed in with his white fur.

Sarah followed her outside and pulled a personal Advanced Radiation Detector out of her pocket. "We haven't had to use this in forever, Dan said, but I paired it with my phone. Let's see what this orange freezie goop is on him."

As Jonah held the cub in his arms, Sarah swept the device over the cub's body in all directions. There was no jump in the digital meter at all.

"Well, the good news is, he's not radioactive. So whatever's been dumped out there isn't going to turn this place into another Chernobyl."

She took the cub from Jonah and stashed it, still wrapped in Kira's parka, inside the cage.

"We have no idea how long the mother has been dead," Kira said. "I put a pile of rocks beside her body, and I'll remember where she is because there was another inukshuk marking that spot, too. We need to go back out there after the blizzard and get her body. I'm going to text you photos of the orange areas on the shore. There was a drum barrel, too, but we didn't stick around because those guys started shooting at us."

Sarah shut the travel crate door and locked it. The bear cub would enjoy his ride to the Polar Bear Jail. "Hey, tell Lukas I hope he recovers quick. We need to get going before the storm hits."

She picked up the handle of the metal trailer and headed over to her truck. The snow blew around her, swirling upwards. Darkness had descended in the short time they'd been talking. Kira shivered and rubbed her upper arms again as she ran back inside. At the cold, and because her beloved town faced an unknown danger no one could've anticipated. She shook off her thoughts. Sarah could worry about the bear cub. For now, all she cared about was Lukas.

CHAPTER 12

L ukas woke with a start. The scent of hot beef and coffee teased his nose. He tested his extremities, and other than the searing pain in his left shoulder and down his arm, everything felt fine. The overhead light shone on Kira's head as she scrolled through her phone. She sat with her left leg scooped underneath her on the chair. Of course she was ignoring her concussion instructions; some things never changed.

Her hair sparkled, swept up in a scrunchie, and he was surprised to see red glasses perched on her nose. He swallowed on a parched throat but tried not to make a sound. He wanted to stare at her forever.

She must've heard him because she turned and smiled.

"How're you feeling?"

She stood and closed the distance from the chair to his hospital bed in one step. He didn't remember moving to a room.

"Guess it's my turn to ask for a drink of water." He made a face. "What'm I doing in here? Thought we were going home."

"A blizzard is coming in, and it's going to hit hard in about an hour. It's already started over the bay. Dr. Stedman figured we might as well spend the night. Ruby and Sophie are doing fine. I already checked in with her."

Kira smiled. His breath hitched in his chest. Loose tendrils of hair fell around her face, and her glasses made her cuter than cute, although he knew she preferred her contacts. He closed his eyes and opened them again for the sheer joy of looking at her. Man, he had it bad. Again.

"Feel like eating? The nurse brought you a tray."

"What about you?" He eyed the covered dishes on the tray.

"I grabbed a sandwich and a couple of chocolate macadamia cookies from the cafeteria. If you want, I can go get you a real coffee."

He hit the bed button to raise the head of the bed. "No, I'm good. That pain shot wore off, but I'm good." He stifled a groan at the bed's movement. "You should've gone back home and stayed safe with Ruby."

Kira pushed the hospital table over his bed and uncovered the dishes.

"I'm not letting you out of my sight. This is still hot, so it should at least taste like beef." She smiled again, a full-on, thousand-kilowatt smile. This was the first time she'd smiled with true joy since he'd found her beside Michael's grave.

I'm not letting you out of my sight.

Well, he wasn't going to let her out of his sight either. His chest squeezed. He should've known it all along. He still loved her. Still wanted her in his life. And he would protect her to his dying breath.

He blinked hard to get his emotions under control.

"Okay, as long as you don't mind me eating in front of you." He winced as he rearranged himself on the bed to reach his food. "Man, I'd hate to know what a bullet in the gut would be like."

She sobered. "You were lucky. I'm so sorry, Lukas. This is all my fault."

He waved his fork at her. "I told you, none of this is your fault."

She pulled the chair over and sat with her feet up on his bedrail.

"You took a bullet for me." Her eyes glistened in the lamplight.

He gave her a cocky grin; at least, he hoped it was a cocky grin. "And I'd take another one for you. Although I never did see the pink elephants Dr. Stedman promised me."

"Oh, you." Kira pitched a magazine at him, laughing, and the tension dissipated.

"Well, Tedford Mines is obviously dumping their toxic waste somehow," she said. "I asked Sarah to get tests run on the ooze samples from the bear cub, but getting the mother bear's body back to the natural resource's headquarters will have to wait till after the blizzard."

Lukas sipped the weak coffee. "And how did he react to your news?"

She propped her chin on her hand. "Ah, he asked me who we'd showed the photos to. I thought that was weird. The ASRC has to inform the natural resource's department and the federal government right away, photos or no photos."

"Kira, till we find those shooters, I don't want you going anywhere alone."

She smiled at him again. "I'm not alone, Lukas; I'm with you."

"I know, you are now, I mean—whenever. At least hang with Eva or someone."

"Done. Of course." She leaned back in the chair and took a deep breath. "I'm so glad Michael kept those emails now. We'll be able to prove what Tedford and Webster Technologies have done and help the RCMP prosecute them." She stopped and smacked her hand on the chair arm. "Should I have said anything about the emails to Professor Birchall? He's got to report this to conservation anyway because of the bear cub..."

"Wait on that," he said. "Let's see how fast he gets the tests run."

Lukas pushed away his empty dishes and moved the hospital table aside. The kidnappers and now these two shooters up here were just hired guns. "Hired by whom" was the question. He didn't have a good reason to ask her to withhold information from her boss, but protecting her from danger was his priority.

Still, sitting up in bed with nothing but bandages around his chest and shoulder, and hospital scrub pants on, he felt a tad vulnerable. Not a nice feeling. *How many times did a security guard come around the ER department per shift?* The room didn't offer much in the way of weapons beyond a kidney-shaped basin and his IV pole.

He tweaked her toes as they rested on the bedrail.

"Hey," she squeaked.

"What's changed your mind about being cooperative?"

"Meaning?"

"You said, *of course,* like I'm a dummy, when I distinctly remember you being pretty *get out of my face* when we were in Winnipeg."

Kira pushed her glasses back up her nose and shrugged. "I'm not an idiot. Those bullets they were shooting at us were real. You bleeding all over the rover was plenty real."

She put her feet on the floor and leaned her forearms on the top bedrail. Then she turned her face towards him. "I'm glad Constable Koper got the Winnipeg police to look at Michael's accident again. They killed Michael to silence him. We just have to figure out *who* killed him, that's all."

The overhead room light flickered several times and then went out. The monitor showing his heart rate and blood pressure went black and fired up again with dimmer readings. In the hallway, the nurses called back and forth to each other.

"What's going on?" Kira went to the door and looked out. "All the lights are out, Lukas."

He pushed down his bedrail and swung his legs over, wincing as his shoulder hit the raised mattress.

"Are you sure?" He looked around for his shoes and socks. "Where are my clothes?" His hospital scrub pants didn't make him feel dressed for action.

A nurse appeared at their door.

"Please stay in your room for your own safety. The power's out because of the storm, but our backup generator will be on soon." Her smile was more plastic than sandwich baggies. "This usually happens at least once a winter." She rushed on to the next room.

Kira turned back to Lukas and shrugged. "I guess we stay put."

Lukas put his hands on the bed. "I should get dressed. What if we have to evacuate?"

"You mean if the heat goes out? I never thought about that," Kira said. "But you have to promise to stay in bed if I give you your clothes back." She had her no-nonsense scientist face on. He almost grinned but held his hands up in mock surrender instead.

"Just my jeans, and socks for my feet, which are freezing anyway. There's only one thin blanket on this bed. I promise to be good."

Kira sniffed but produced his clothes from a locker he hadn't even noticed in the far corner.

"I'm going to try to call Eva, so I'll be within shouting distance if you need me."

He nodded absent-mindedly and grabbed his clothes from her. She pulled the door shut behind her.

When she returned, she carried a small, battery-operated lamp. "The nurse at the station gave me this so we can see what we're doing." She sat the lamp on the bedside table.

"What happened with the generator?"

"She said they're still working on it, but there's something wrong," Kira said.

"Guess we're stuck then."

"Guess we are," she said. She smoothed the blanket back over his legs and tucked it in around him.

"I'm a sucker for a pretty nurse."

She blushed so pink he could see the bloom on her cheeks even in the dim light. She gave his knees a smack on the blanket and pulled the chair closer to the bed so she could put her arms on the bedrail again.

Lukas caressed her cheek with his first knuckle. Her skin was as soft as Sophie's.

"You and Ruby were having an intense discussion the other night."

Kira shifted away from his hand. "Not really."

"No?" He set his hand on top of the covers. Her lips tightened, just a fleeting micro-expression.

"She's a solid friend to us. I wouldn't have made it after..." he paused, "after Abby died if Ruby hadn't stepped up to help me with Sophie."

Kira stared at a spot on his bed blanket.

133

"You can trust her, Kira."

"Yeah, I know." She shifted back into the chair, settling away from him. He felt her warmth withdraw. He'd struck a nerve. Other than the occasional footfalls of the nurse outside his room and the odd phone ringing, the hall was quiet.

"You know you can trust me, too, right?" He shifted against the sheets to get into a more comfortable position. The painkiller shot had worn off fast. The full-bore, fiery pain enveloped his entire left arm.

Now, she was avoiding his gaze and staring at the far wall.

"Kira, please look at me. And don't even think about going out that door."

Her head whipped around so fast he thought she'd cracked her neck. Those deep hazel eyes sparked behind her glasses, and her ponytail smacked against her cheek.

"I'm far from being the kid I was five years ago, Lukas." Her hands gripped the armrests of the chair, her feet planted side by side.

"Kira, please." He raised his hands again in the universal surrender position. "I don't want to fight with you. I want to understand..." Suddenly, he couldn't go on. He swallowed, emotion flushing his cheeks. "I *need* to understand. What went wrong that night at The Dove?"

She bent over and yanked on her winter boots, shoving her feet into them. He leaned over as much as he could.

"Kira, don't do this," he rasped. Not good, it hurt to move that way. He sat back, his heart thudding in his chest, breathing hard.

She stared at the floor, her hands still on the armrests. Now he could just see the top of her head.

"I'm sorry," she whispered, "you deserve to know." She raised her head and looked at him. Tears rolled down her cheeks. "After all, you just took a bullet for me."

She put her hand on the bedrail, and he covered it with his right hand. She wiped her tears with her other hand and pulled the chair in a bit closer.

"Is this what you were talking to Ruby about?" he asked.

She nodded.

"Okay then. I'll listen, and I promise not to say a word till you're finished."

"No matter what?"

"No matter what."

He tightened his hand over hers and rubbed his thumb along the top of her hand. His stomach flipped ice cubes as he took a deep breath.

"You're not going to like it."

"I can take it, Kira."

"That last winter in university," the tears rolled faster over her chin, "I did a stupid thing."

She hesitated.

He squeezed her hand.

"I showered in the common bathroom and left my room door unlocked." She swallowed. "I didn't, you know, pay attention to my surroundings when I got back to my room like they told us in orientation..."

Lukas swore he could hear a faint bell clanging away in the distance. Since when did the hospital have a bell? Or was it in his mind?

Kira squared her shoulders. "There was a guy hiding in my room. He had a knife. And... he said he'd kill me..."

The bell in his mind rang louder, slow gonging sounds, cracking against the sides of his head. Kira spoke, but he couldn't take in her words. Her eyes were on their entwined hands, her tears falling, splashing on their fingers.

He stared at their hands while images ran in front of his eyes. Kira, losing weight, shrinking in her clothes till she looked tiny in her class chair. Kira, eyes smudged with dark circles, never smiling. Why hadn't he questioned her? Why hadn't he paid more attention?

He said he'd kill me...

Lukas swallowed bile at the back of his throat. He'd missed all the signs. When she ran away, he'd let his father make up his mind for him. "Let her run, son. She's got no staying power. Not the kind you need in your life."

Lukas rubbed gentle circles over the top of her cold hand.

"Why didn't you say anything? Did you report it? Do you know who it was?"

His head felt cleaved in two. Pain jagged through his brain. He struggled to sit upright so he could reach her, hold her.

"How could I tell you how stupid I'd been?"

"Kira, you weren't stupid."

"Yeah? You say that now." She stared at the wall. "Back then, you liked things to be perfect. I had a lot to live up to."

He groaned. *Oh Lord, she's right. Kira, can you watch how you open the car door? You never take care of anything you own; don't you realize how much things cost? Kira, you've put a rip in the leather on my steering wheel!*

"Kira, it's all right. I'm sorry if I made you feel that way..."

"It'll never be all right!" Her voice cracked. "I'll always be the damaged goods your father used to call me."

"Kira, Kira, please," was all he could say. His voice sounded like a faraway echo.

She pulled her hand away. He cringed under her furious eyes. Her face was stark under the dim, bluish light.

"Yes."

One word. A bare whisper.

"I know who it was... It was Derek Straughn. From my chemistry class."

She stepped back and blew her nose, hunching her shoulders away from him.

"And I did report it, for all the good it did me."

"But why didn't you tell *me*? I was your boyfriend; you should've told me."

She looked over her shoulder. Shock shone in her eyes, and her mouth opened slightly. He'd put his foot in it but didn't understand how.

"Why, because you thought I belonged to you? Like your fancy sports car?"

"That's not what I meant, and you know it."

"Yeah, so what did you mean then?"

She shoved the tissue in her jeans pocket. He knew that rebellious look on her face. Part anger, part defense, it was pure Kira 101. How had he forgotten her hard outer shell?

A sharp knock sounded on his door. Kira turned towards the window, crossing her arms over her chest.

"Come in," Lukas called.

Corporal Mackenzie came around the door and glanced over at Kira's rigid back. He raised an eyebrow at Lukas as he said, "Good time or bad time?"

Lukas held his breath for a count of four seconds and released it for four seconds. He thinned his lips.

"It's fine. What's up?"

"Wanted to see how you're doing. How's the shoulder?"

"Good. I can go home after the storm's over." Lukas shifted to get comfortable again. "What's that you've got there?"

Mackenzie came fully into the small room and laid a box of ammunition and a ballistic vest on the over-the-bed table, along with some plastic zip ties.

"We brought your truck into town for you. It's out in the parking lot. And your rifle's out on the back rack of your truck." He paused while he took off his heavy gloves. "We chased that snowmobile all over town but lost it out by the old military base. Then when we decided to check the port granaries again, another snowmobile appeared, a red one this time, and they started shooting at Sarah Thorvald and her partner. I can't have strangers driving around town shooting at people, but I'm only one guy."

He glanced over at Kira's back again before continuing. "Then within the past hour, someone emptied all seven bears out of the Polar Bear Jail. Sarah and her partner are out patrolling to try to find them, because that's a lot of bears roaming in town. The storm's hitting, and who knows where the bears will try to hunker down to wait it out. It's a dangerous situation."

Lukas stared at the box of ammunition. "But why bring me my ammo in here?"

Mackenzie took a deep breath. "Well, I spoke to Ben who's just out of surgery upstairs. He vouched for you. He's out of commission, and I can't be everywhere. It's unorthodox, and I wouldn't do this for just anyone. But, the criminal code allows citizens to make an arrest if they find someone committing a crime." He narrowed his eyes as he put his hands on his hips to stare at Lukas. "Those plastic zip ties are to use, should you have occasion to make a citizen's arrest of anyone who's shooting at you. And according to the criminal code, you have to turn that person or persons over to me at the earliest possible opportunity."

"Okay," Lukas drew out the word, "and thanks for the ballistic vest, I guess."

"I think Kira should wear it, actually. They're coming after her, although Jonah tells me she knows her way around a shotgun. Maybe she can keep yours close by till we get these guys."

At that, Kira turned from the window. Her face shone pale under the light.

"Thank you, Corporal Mackenzie. I appreciate you thinking of me." She glanced over at the equipment.

"Another thing. The forensics finally came back on the café explosion. Just a homemade C4 bomb on a cell phone timer. Anyone could've made it from instructions on the internet. Still, it's a good thing it was small and mainly took out the front half of the building."

Lukas glanced at Kira's white face. She shivered.

"How bad is the storm now?" she asked.

"Starting to whip up pretty good. It'll be a whiteout soon." He straightened his hat. "You two stay put. Things should look better in the morning, noon at the latest."

"Thanks, I can pay you back for it." Lukas nodded towards the box of bullets.

Mackenzie grinned. "No worries. I want everyone to stay safe. Have a good night, folks." He waved as he left the room.

Silence filled the tiny room and shoved against the walls. Lukas cleared his throat, but Kira cut him off.

"I need to try Eva again, so I'll just go out in the hall." Her head down, she patted her pockets. "I've got my phone, keys, and wallet. Need anything from the vending machines?"

"I'm good," he said.

"Fine, I'll be right back."

She was quickly out the door, pulling it shut behind her. At least she hadn't run out the door. He leaned back against the pillow, massaging his pounding forehead. What was wrong with him? *He was her boyfriend, so she had to tell him?* She'd been through a major life-and-death trauma, and he hadn't even picked up on the signals. His life, his studies, his new job, they'd been the important things pervading his thoughts. What kind of *boyfriend* did that make him?

He'd deserved to lose her. He'd been a complete idiot.

His IV stand was on rollers. He didn't need the vest and ammo in here, but he could at least follow her out into the hall to keep an eye on her. He would never let her down ever again. He found his boots and shoved his feet in them. Never again.

CHAPTER 13

Kira punched the buttons in the vending machine for two chocolate bars. They didn't fall, so she slammed the flat of her hand against the front of it. She felt like smashing some more vending machines. A whole row of vending machines.

All those clichés rolled through her mind: feeling a load off her shoulders, a weight off her chest, even no more butterflies in her stomach. She'd finally, finally told Lukas her secret. It was out there. No taking it back.

But all she felt was starving.

Still no chocolate bars. She slammed the machine again. One bar fell, but the other one sat halfway out of its metal coil, taunting her. She could lie to herself and say that one was for Lukas, but no, she planned on munching her way through both of those confections of sugary chocolate, caramel, and peanuts. One more smack, and the candy bar dropped to the bottom. She fished it out, bending her arm backwards.

They must've gotten the generator going because the ceiling lights were about 50 percent strength. They cast a bluish light over the nurses' faces as they scurried about doing their jobs. The light faded to black at the extreme ends of the corridor, and she kept her head on a swivel as she let the exquisite mixture of chocolate and caramel roll over her tongue. So delicious, but she knew she'd get a monster sugar headache.

She thought she'd feel relieved to have the big reveal over, but all she felt was hollow. Empty. As if her dire secret had filled her core and been such a huge part of her, she was now an empty husk. She shoved the thought away while she crumpled the wrappers and threw them in the garbage pail beside the vending machine.

Her head pounded with a vengeance. Concussion or sugar headache? Right now, she didn't care.

Kira pulled out her phone and hit speed dial for the ASRC.

"Eva?" An orderly gave her a look as he passed her. Guess her voice was too loud.

"Hey, Kira." Background voices rose and fell, laughter and dishes clinking.

"Listen, what's up with Birchall?" Kira leaned against the vending machine. "He didn't seem too concerned about the hazardous waste or my bear cub's health."

Kira could hear muffled sounds as if Eva had her hand over the receiver. Eva cleared her throat. "Professor Birchall has a couple of things on the go. He just wants you back at work, that's all."

"It's *probably hazardous waste—maybe even toxic waste,* Eva! Is everything all right out there? You didn't call me back when I left you that message," Kira said.

Silence. Profound silence.

"Eva, you realize you can talk to me. I'm your team leader, and I'm here to help you."

"There's something wrong with his stepson, Avery Scott," Eva whispered.

"Like what? Is he ill?"

"No, I don't know." Eva must have put her hand over the phone again; she could hear muffled scratching. "It's bad, Kira. Birchall's got a cell phone locked in his desk, and he uses it to only talk to Avery. Isn't that kind of weird?"

She paused. "Yeah, a little bit. Do you think that's why Birchall's not acting like himself?"

"Whenever you get back, I can tell you more," Eva whispered.

"I don't know when that will be, but I'll keep in touch," Kira said.

Lukas appeared beside her, his hand resting on the vending machine beside her head. He'd thrown his flannel shirt on over his bandaged shoulder and chest and shoved his jeans into his winter boots. The emergency lights cast swarthy shadows over his face, accentuating the hard planes of his cheeks and beard stubble. Harsh but handsome beard stubble. Kira swore the air closed in around them till all she could feel was his body warmth. His breath smelled of cinnamon gum.

"I gotta go, Eva. Text me if something comes up and you need to talk."

"I will; I promise."

Kira hesitated as she looked up at Lukas. She could see from his eyes he was due for another painkiller, yet his gaze on her held compassion. She struggled to come up with something intelligent to say. Or anything at all.

"You okay?" he asked.

She offered him the last bite of her chocolate bar. "I'm better than okay," she said. His remarks still stung, but she grabbed on to her common sense. Her goal had been to tell him her secret, and she'd done that—what he did with the information was up to him.

A shriek pierced the air behind the double doors at the far end of the hallway. A nurse tore past them to the sound. Lukas grabbed Kira and pulled her to his chest. The double doors burst open, and people came rushing towards them.

Firecrackers–again. Not firecrackers, bullets. More screams.

The flow of people from the ER crushed them against the vending machine and cut them off from Lukas's room. The edge of the vending machine dug into Kira's spine.

"I should've brought you the vest out of my room," Lukas said.

"I didn't think I'd need it out here," she said. "All I wanted was a chocolate bar."

Lukas tore his IV from his arm.

"No," Kira cried. "What are you doing?"

He grabbed her hand and pulled her in the direction the people were running. "This is no time to be a hero," he said. "I'm getting you out of here."

They charged down the hall, going with the crowd. A gurney came out of nowhere and plowed into them as several more people ran by. It pinned Lukas against the wall, and Kira lost her hold on him. She fell to her knees and scrambled on all fours towards the nursing station in the center of the corridor.

"Lukas? Are you okay?"

She pulled herself into a ball behind the half-circular desk. One more person ran by and out the end of their corridor. She could hear someone sobbing off to her right side.

"Kira, shush." His tone was harsh. Oh yes, he sounded fine. "Call 911 if you have your phone."

She slapped her thigh pockets, trying to find her phone. "It's not here. I must've dropped it."

"Can you reach the desk phone?"

The double doors creaked at the ER end of the hallway where the shooting had come from, and she froze in place. She was a sitting duck underneath the desk. She needed to be in a room, barricaded if possible. And Lukas wasn't in her line of sight. She couldn't tell where he was, even from his voice. Her head rang, blood rushing in her ears. Was he still to her left? She pressed her lips together with her hand so her breathing couldn't be heard.

Another creak. *One-one thousand, two-one thousand, three-one thousand.* She counted until she heard the next creaking noise. She had no idea how many feet long the corridor was, but it gave her an idea how far away the shooter was from the nurse's station. Each count of one-one thousand was a second between the creaks. She eased her feet out from under her and got into a crouching position.

Every one of her five senses telescoped. Her self-defense training morphed into the forefront of her mind. Adrenaline poured through her

143

blood, bringing energy and strength to her muscles. She backed up and moved a desk chair to the side so she had room to move in case the gunman appeared over the counter. Her thigh muscles screamed while she held her position.

One more noise, a soft padding sound to her immediate left. The person came inside her perimeter, inside the desk area. Kira pivoted and rose upwards, her left hand grabbing the barrel of the gun aimed down at her. Her right hand punched her assailant in the throat, connecting in a solid strike to his flesh.

Oomph.

Just as her brain registered triumph, a shadowy figure to her right stabbed the side of her neck with a needle. The flood of chemicals into her bloodstream raced hot throughout her body and shot up to her brain. Then all went black.

The front side of Kira's body boiled, but her back was freezing cold. Her face burned like her skin would peel off in layers. Her eyelids puffed out, and grit glued them together. Inch by inch, feeling came screaming back into her body—she lay on a metal frame bed, with metal springs and no mattress, in front of a roaring fire.

Kira struggled to open her eyes but could only lift her eyelashes a fraction of an inch. Just enough to see the fire crackling in some kind of furnace. Her backside was freezing; her captors hadn't covered her up. She lay on her left side, her left wrist and ankle handcuffed and chained to the metal cot. Her regular blouse and jeans were no match for the deep, subarctic temperatures of the blizzard outside or the lack of heat in back of her... wherever this was. She couldn't turn her head.

Someone stood in her right peripheral vision, and several voices muttered in the room, but no one paid her any attention. She shivered— a deep, visceral shiver. She had no feeling in her fingers and toes. Frostbite wouldn't be far behind. In contrast, small areas blistered with heat along her cheeks.

"Why did you bring her here, of all places?"

She knew the voice. An older woman's voice.

"Thought you wanted an easy way to dispose of her. There's barrels of ways to dispose of her in here."

A different voice. A woman's voice far away.

"And why didn't you bring all her clothes?"

"There was no time to grab her stuff." Groggy, she tried to place the man's voice as well. "There was nothing else in his hospital room. We've searched everywhere. You want to find it, you're going to have to use extreme measures."

"Oh, I'm going to have to use extreme measures? What's wrong with you? I thought you were the expert."

Kira tried to shift backwards to get away from the heat, but her jeans caught on the metal springs of the bed. One jabbed her in the thigh through her jeans. She stifled a cry.

Extreme measures? They were talking like this was a TV show. But they were looking for the flash drive—which she didn't have with her. How long could she last under *extreme measures?*

Her tongue adhered to the roof of her mouth. She was sure the guy talking had taken a hammer and split her head in two. And she desperately had to use the facilities.

God, please help me! Protect me and help Lukas to find me.

She pressed her legs together, rattling the chain. She moved her right hand over her lips, face, and eyes. No abrasions or bleeding, so that was good. She concentrated on breathing quietly and opening her swollen eyes enough to see who was talking.

"She's already told the cops. Who cares if we don't find the flash drive?"

That snotty tone... now she knew the voice. A younger female than the first one.

"Because the flash drive is primary evidence, you useless twit." A chair scraped. "It doesn't matter what she's told the cops. They need proper evidence to prove it."

Alison Webster. That slightly nasal, Eastern twang. What was she doing here with two hired thugs? Kira tried to swallow, but her mouth couldn't work up enough saliva. She inhaled and banged her head on the metal bed, coughing and sputtering.

"She's awake already?" The young woman's legs came into Kira's view. Black snow pants and boots. The woman squatted down so her face was on the same level. Well, surprise, surprise. Violet-haired Chelsea from Ruby's Café and Emporium.

"Where's the flash drive?" Chelsea shoved Kira's forehead backwards with her palm. "We don't have time to play nicey-nice. Hand it over, and we all go home."

"Yeah, right," Kira croaked out. "You're going to put me in a barrel. A nice cocktail of arsenic, lead, and maybe mercury."

"My dear Kira," Alison said, "just give it to us, and I promise no one's going to put you in a barrel of anything."

"I don't have it here, but I can give it to you if you take me back to town."

"She's bluffing," Chelsea said. "We've torn your place apart. You have to have it, so get ready to be body searched, because we don't have all night to sit here in a blizzard."

"That won't be necessary," the man said. "She'll give it to us. Won't you, Kira?"

Goose bumps rose on Kira's arms. So unexpected. So unbelievable. She refused to look at him.

The man motioned Chelsea aside, then squatted down beside the cot. "Just give it to us, Kira. I promise we won't hurt you."

She slid further back on the metal cot, ignoring the coil piercing her jeans into her thigh. Her hand at her throat, she squinted at the man through her tears. She shook her head.

"I don't have it. Please—let me go." She bit her bottom lip, her body quaking on the metal bed.

The man drew out a hunting knife. It's razor sharp edge glinted in the fire light. He scratched a line of red dots, blood springing up from her wrist to her elbow from the knife cuts.

"This is your last chance, Kira," Jonah said.

CHAPTER 14

Lukas fought the steering wheel all the way down the road. A nurse had zipped up his parka, securing his useless left arm underneath. He peered ahead into the blinding snow flying against his windshield. His headlights were the only light for miles. Once he found the turnoff to his house, he wrenched on the wheel again, bumping against ruts and struggling to stay on track.

His loaded rifle and shotgun lay in the rack behind him in case he came across one of those seven bears. The townspeople had heeded the radio warnings to stay indoors, and the streets stood empty all the way from the hospital to the barren flats heading to his property. He glanced down at his phone as he pulled up to the barn. The "Little Lamb" tracker chip he'd put in Kira's boots a few days ago wasn't lighting up. Either she was more than a mile away or somewhere there was no cell signal.

He tried to ring Corporal Mackenzie again, but his call went straight to voicemail.

"Hey, Kira's been kidnapped, and I have no idea where she is... call me when you get this message!"

A shudder went through him. Someone had managed to kidnap Kira a second time. In a blizzard. He could see his house was in darkness. Only the foyer night light was on. Sophie and Ruby must be asleep.

Lukas pulled his parka hood tighter around his face. He bailed out of the truck, running through drifting snow towards the house. The snow was blowing in from the northwest and coming across his property on a diagonal. He leaned into it to get to the front deck, scrabble his way up the stairs and across to the front door.

Claw-like, his fingers managed to key the lock, his breath freezing on his parka hood's fur. Just as he turned the key, the door gave way, and he fell forwards into Ruby's arms.

"Sophie?"

Ruby tightened her arms around him, then helped him sit down on the foyer floor. She closed the front door against the blowing snow.

"She's sound asleep. Why aren't you in the hospital?"

"They took Kira." He struggled to his knees and then to his feet, putting a hand on the wall. "I have to get her back. Now."

"Who took Kira? Where's Corporal Mackenzie?" Ruby followed him to his bedroom door, clutching her robe about her neck. "You can barely stand."

"No time." Lukas unzipped his parka, dropping it to the floor where he stood. "Where's my snowmobile suit?" He wavered on his feet in front of his closet.

"Not in there, that's for certain." Ruby headed back to the laundry room. "You look weak enough to be back in bed. You got shot today, or didn't you get the memo?"

His phone started beeping—a high-pitched chirping. He grabbed it from his jeans pocket and stabbed the red circle.

"It's working!"

"What's working?"

"She's alive!" He thrust the phone at Ruby. "She's at the Granaries. She's on the move."

Lukas took the one-piece snowmobile suit from her and sat on his bed.

"I've got to get her back."

"That's what the police are for—"

"I failed her once, Ruby. I'm not failing her again."

With his right hand, he yanked it on over his feet, hopped up, and hiked it over his hips and wiggled it up so that his right arm was in the sleeve. With his left arm bandaged to his chest, he turned to Ruby.

"Zip me up, will you?"

She blew out a breath. "You are one stubborn, stubborn man. You're not doing her any good going off on a snowmobile in this blizzard." But she zipped up the suit and the neck zippers. She stepped back and patted him on the chest. "There. How're you going to steer a snowmobile with only one arm?"

"I'm not. I'm taking the dogs."

With that, he left her standing with her mouth open and headed out into the freezing storm.

Kira cracked her neck on each side and rolled her shoulders, loosening her back bones between them. "Not too shabby for someone who can't dress her own deer, eh? Didn't expect me to have a green belt, did you, sweetheart?" Adrenaline buzzed through her system. She hopped from foot to foot as Chelsea glared at her from where she lay on the floor.

Kira bent down and finished tying Chelsea's wrists to the metal legs of the shelving unit in the dank storage room Jonah had locked them in for her "body search." Twisting her body, Chelsea tried one last time to kick Kira but missed.

Kira stood and rubbed her raw knuckles. "I told you to stay down. You should've listened."

She ignored the girl's cursing and scanned the shelves for any chemicals she could use as a weapon. She didn't see anything stronger than Lysol, although she could always try to toss it in Jonah's or Alison's eyes if she got a chance. No windows for an escape, and no blankets for warmth. She scooted down on her haunches against the opposite wall and stared at Chelsea.

"How did you get mixed up in this mess?"

Chelsea cocked an eyebrow under her violet bangs and yanked on her plastic ties. "Like you care."

Kira shrugged. "You're right. I don't." She scanned the cement block walls of the room again, but there was no way out. "Just wondering why someone who'd grown up here would go along with poisoning your own environment."

"I'm not planning to stay here." Chelsea twisted her wrists against the ties till her skin turned red. "Let me go. Jonah's going to make short work of you."

Kira stood and moved some boxes piled in the opposite corner. She glanced over her shoulder now and then to keep an eye on Chelsea.

"So you keep saying." She brushed the dirt off her hands. "I'm more interested in how you got hooked up with him and the Queen of Toxic Waste. Hasn't Ruby treated you right?"

Chelsea's glare could've peeled wallpaper off the wall, had there been any on the cement walls. "Minimum wage isn't going to get me south. Avery and I have plans... we want a real life, not be stuck up here on the tundra forever."

"So, it's money and true love. How did a girl like you meet Avery Scott?"

"Like I'd tell you."

Kira snorted. "Okay then, Miss Criminal Mastermind, how much is kidnapping and murder worth these days? Because on top of the muck on the shore I saw, you're going down for what you've done to me tonight." She pointed to her swollen eyes and the right side of her face. "You're an accomplice, and you've kidnapped me. You plan on killing me to shut me up. So I do hope Mrs. Webster out there is paying you enough."

Chelsea skidded forward on her bottom, thrashing her legs at Kira's and connecting with her right ankle in a scissor kick.

Kira cried out and stomped on the girl's foot. She threw herself backwards against the wall to stop herself from continuing to pummel the teenager. Holding her knees, bent over, she drew in deep, gulping breaths.

The metal door of the storage room flew open. Jonah filled the opening, his shoulders touching the door frame on each side. He twisted Kira's left ear and brought her outside the room into the hallway. She clawed at his hand, even though she knew he could control her with that hold. He shoved the door shut on Chelsea's screams of profanity and demands to let her out.

"You really are more trouble than you're worth." He hauled her up by the back of her belt, which kept her off balance, while maintaining his grip on her ear. "I should've known you could take Chelsea one on one."

"I can take you, too," Kira spat out, "if I could trust you not to call in one of those thugs in the other room."

Jonah jerked her upright so her face was inches from his. In the fluorescent light of the granary, his face loomed like a mask of jagged rock. His gaze bored black holes into hers, and she shivered. *Those eyes. Derek's eyes. Both furious men, both seeking power over her.*

"Where is the flash drive? This is your last chance, Kira, or you give me no choice."

"So kill me then. Like you did my brother." She tried to move, but his strong hand held her fast by the back of her neck, his fingers closing around the sides of her throat. He drew her face closer still.

"Your brother thought he was so much better than me. But Avery drove him off the road." He paused. His breath hot and sticky on her face made her gag.

Avery? Professor Birchall's stepson?

"Avery's seventeen. Since when does he own a brand-new truck?" Kira forced the words out through clenched teeth.

"Since step-daddy indulges his every whim. Who knew the kid could drive so fast? Took care of business, for once in his pathetic life."

People rounded the corner behind them, and he shifted his body weight to bring her closer to him. To hide her face?

"I told you, I'm not going to be a party to murder. You'll have to figure out a better way to dispose of her than a barrel of toxic waste."

A loud, hacking cough. "You were supposed to come up with a cover story!"

Kira stiffened, her heart pounding. Another male voice she knew. How many shocks could she handle in one night?

"There's no time for that. The plane leaves as soon as the storm clears. I suggest you use the fact you'll be debt free to salve your conscience," Alison said. "You do want to be on the plane, don't you?"

Kira stomped on Jonah's foot with all her weight, making him loosen his grip and cry out. She shoved away from his body and ran down the opposite end of the hallway towards the only door she could see. As she did so, the shocked looks on the faces of Alison Webster and Ian Birchall loomed in her vision like scary clowns in a fun house mirror.

She ran pell-mell down the cement hall with Jonah fast behind her. Adrenaline flooded her veins, and her legs pumped. But he threw himself on her, and her shoulder cracked against the metal door. She slid down the door into a twisted heap with Jonah on top of her.

"That," he panted, "is the last time you will make me run."

He yanked her arms behind her, fastening them with plastic ties. He sat on her lower legs while he caught his breath. Then he hauled her upright and, putting his arm through her restraints, dragged her by her elbows, to where the two bosses stood.

"She doesn't have it on her." He blew out his breath. "We're wasting time. If the cop even has a copy, there's no way we can counteract that, so I suggest you make up your minds about what to do with her."

Alison's bright grey eyes peered at Kira. She frowned and tapped one red nail on her lips. "Oh, my dear, such a mess of a pretty face. Whatever are we going to do with you?"

Kira swung her battered face over to her boss. "How could you? How could you do this to the bay, the polar bears?"

She saw raw fear and something else in his eyes. Anger, sorrow. They flitted over his face and disappeared. "My boy Avery needs rehab. The government doesn't pay for the kind of excellent programming he requires. And my online gambling has gotten... a bit beyond me." He straightened. "None of which is any of your business."

"How could you dump a barrel on the shore like that?"

Jonah yanked on her ponytail, making her eyes water.

"What do you care?" he snarled. "You ask too many questions."

Kira squirmed till she could look at Birchall. "You're lucky the permafrost is completely frozen right now. We might have a chance to clean that mess up. What about the birds and small animals? What about the polar bears? The mercury and lead will kill them eventually. How could you wreck this place—for gambling debts?" She grabbed at Jonah's hands fisted in her hair. "Let me go!"

"Or what?" Jonah pulled her to him, his breath hot on her ear. "You should worry about your own life, not about the stupid polar bears." He twisted her backwards like a bow. "I hate save-the-animal freaks."

"There's no need for violence, Mr. Adams," Birchall said. "Kira, you'd do well to give up the flash drive. Michael died for nothing. Is that what you want? Once the sea ice forms in another week and the bears head out to feed on the seals, this will all blow over."

Jonah let her fall forward. She tripped but steadied herself in front of her boss.

"You're delusional," she said. "That hazardous waste could be concentrated by freezing over the winter—we don't know enough about it. Who knows what damage it'll cause to the animal population or even humans?"

Birchall turned to Alison. "She could come with us."

"No!" Alison and Jonah said at the same time.

Kira shuddered.

"No," Alison said after a knowing look at Jonah. "Our Kira knows too much. She won't be happy living in a tropical paradise. She quite obviously loves these stupid polar bears beyond reason." Alison made a wide theatrical gesture. "You should've done a better job on the fire and killed her then."

"There're lots of barrels in the other room with her name on them," Jonah said.

"Absolutely not," Birchall said.

"What then?" Jonah strode towards him, keeping Kira strapped to his side. Birchall shrank into his parka. "It's time to go. There's no more time to waste, so figure it out."

Kira's legs shook uncontrollably. There was no feeling in her fingers or toes.

Lord, please don't let me die tonight.

She peered at Birchall through her swollen eyes. Her stomach churned as he stared hard at her.

"Professor..."

"Not so snarky now, are we?" Jonah laughed. "She loves her polar bears so much, she can spend her last hours with them. Drive her out on the tundra and leave her in the snow."

"What? Are you nuts?" said Birchall.

Jonah tightened his grip on Kira's neck. "Trust me, it's a merciful death. She'll either freeze to death or a bear will find her. Either way, her blood's not on our hands."

Birchall turned to Alison. "You can't be okay with this crazy idea."

"Why not? Let nature take its course." She pulled up her parka hood. "Just make sure you get to the airport in plenty of time. That plane won't wait." She tipped up Kira's chin to look her in the eyes. "It's just business, my dear. It's not personal. Not with Michael either. He couldn't leave well enough alone."

"But what made you do this? Ruin this beautiful place?"

Alison sighed. "My husband died, leaving the company ten million dollars in debt. And when Tedford Mines approached me with their little toxic waste problem, they were happy to bail Webster Technologies out." She smiled, her small, even, white teeth showing. "Michael figured out the payment code. I couldn't have him going to the police."

"I'd be careful what you say," Jonah said. "Her body search didn't quite go as planned. She could have a recorder on her."

Alison waved a thin hand in the air. "I'm not worried. Avery let all those polar bears out of their jail tonight. I'm sure she'll be busy making sure she's not a meal." She cupped her hand around Kira's bruised cheek. "Goodbye, my dear. Too bad you didn't go back to Winnipeg when your room was destroyed."

Muffled yelling came from the storage room. Alison and Birchall moved down the hallway, leaving Jonah and Kira standing alone. He stood her up by the shoulders and forced her to look at him.

"This isn't my choice, but you should've cooperated. Try anything before we get out there, and I'll kill you." He gave her a small shake. "Nod to show you understand."

Kira moved her head up and down.

"Good, let's go."

He hauled her down the hall and out the metal door, into the swirling, blinding snow.

CHAPTER 15

Lukas's dog team raced onwards through the ebony darkness, the sled whistling against the fresh snow. He kept his eye on the red dot blinking on the map on his cell phone strapped to the front bar of the sled. Once he'd realized Kira's tracker had moved from the port granaries, he'd mushed the dogs easterly towards the Wildlife Management Area.

His fur-lined trapper hat held icicles around his eyes, but his breath fanned warm against the balaclava covering the bottom half of his face. Timber, his lead dog, ran without effort and responded to his weight moving side to side on the sled. His stomach curdled—what if he was wrong about Kira's tracking device? If she was still at the granaries, he was wasting precious time in the blizzard.

Snow whirled around him like ballerinas, circling towards him and then backing away. He could only stare at the red dot moving farther eastward and keep the dogs trained in that direction.

Lord, I was so stupid. I was so caught up in myself, I didn't pay enough attention to Kira or what changes she was going through. I was selfish. I cared too much for my precious car and possessions and not enough about her. If You hadn't given me Abby, I never would've learned how to love a real person. Please let me find Kira. I can't lose her again. I swear I'll love her the right way this time. Please God, help me find her alive.

The eight dogs didn't mind the storm in the least. They enjoyed a good run.

He'd lost all sense of time in the dark.

Hang on, Kira. I'm coming for you, love. Just hang on.

Jonah brought his truck to a standstill, his headlights shining a few feet through the blinding snow. The snow blew so steady it felt like a wall against them as they exited the truck. Kira braced herself in front of the headlights.

"Do you know where you are?"

Dressed only in her blouse, jeans, and boots, she shivered and tried to shove him away.

"Why don't you get on with it?"

"You're going to walk away. Whatever happens to you, it'll be nature taking you out. Not us."

Kira wheezed, her arms crossed against her chest, every cell of her being reacting to the extreme cold.

"Coward." Between her swollen eyes and the spiraling snow, she couldn't see. "You're all cowards. This isn't over."

He laughed deep in his throat. "Do you see the tundra? I think it's over, Kira."

Wind howled in a circle against the truck and blew snow away from in front of the headlights. Kira spotted the bear tracks at the same time Jonah did. Huge, clawed tracks. Deep and full. At least ten inches across. They were going in a diagonal direction across the front of the truck and off into the distance.

She couldn't hold back a gasp even as her knees gave way and she sank to the ground. Jonah yanked her upright.

"I may be a coward, but I'm also a gambler. I'm willing to give you a fighting chance." He handed her his hunting knife, the one he'd used on her forearm. "Take it. It'll even your odds." He reached into the front seat and threw a jacket at her. "Here you go."

Kira's eyelashes held crusted ice particles, her breath frosted against her cheeks. She pulled the jacket on around her shoulders but couldn't zip it. Her bound hands loosely grasped the knife hilt. She stood wobbling side to side, then staggered towards the end of the beam from the truck's headlights. The polar bear tracks went off to the left. Kira sucked frigid air deep into her lungs. She swung to the right and forced her boots forwards.

One step. Another step. She leaned into the wind, the jacket flapping and her blouse molded to her body. The truck backed up, and the light disappeared.The sound of the truck was swallowed up into the whirling snow. Silence. She knew she needed to carve out a shelter, but the bear tracks. What to do about the bear tracks?

Dear God, protect me! I need Your help. I don't want to die.

Pure inky blackness surrounded her. The snow tasted fresh and sharp on her tongue. She turned in a circle, keeping one boot facing forward. She tried to see downward to find the tracks, but the snow blocked her vision. Seven bears had been let out of the jail that evening. One polar bear had crossed here. One would be all it took to kill her. Still, her need for shelter was greater than worrying about a bear attack.

I'm not dying out here, not tonight.

She felt clumsy, dizzy; hypothermia would set in soon. Forcing herself to take a few more steps forwards, she fell flat on her face.

Dig, Kira!

One push, then another, and the knife cut into the snow. She raised herself up on her arms and tried again. Stab, stab, stab.

Lord, I need to tell Lukas... I need to tell him I never stopped loving him.

The snow blew into her mouth, allowing ice shards to pierce her tongue.

Kira, dig!

Lukas? She must be delirious. Snow covered her, how could she dig? So soft, so warm. She was sinking into sleep. Precious sleep...

Dig, Kira!

She woke with a start. Afraid she'd frozen to the ground, she heard the unmistakable sound of a polar bear moving not fifteen feet from her. It gave a low moaning sound deep in its throat as it padded past her in the storm. She could smell its raw, animal scent across the wind. Could it smell her? Heart pounding in her ears, she lay motionless even after she could no longer hear or smell it. But the adrenaline gave her enough energy to draw lines from one stab mark to another in the snow with the knife.

Kira carved an outline around her body and rolled over to one side. The snow still fell in sheets, but she scraped a hollow out of her body shape and shoved the snow into a windbreak against the direction of the snowfall. It wasn't much, but it was all she could do. She packed more snow around her and left a breathing hole.

Lord, it's just You and me out here now. Thank you for bringing Lukas back into my life, for the chance to tell him the truth about why I ran away from him. I know You never left me like I thought you did all those years. I'm so sorry I wasted all that time, and I lost Michael, too. Lord, please take care of Lukas and precious little Sophie. Help her grow up strong and loving, and to know her mother. Help Lukas raise her up to know You. Lord, you don't make mistakes, and she is a beautiful, wonderful little girl. Thank you, God.

She gripped the knife handle and fought the sleep closing in around her. Morning would come.

The dogs kept up their pace across the tundra, but maybe he should hole up from the blizzard. He'd followed the red dot, and now it seemed to be stationary, but it was in the middle of nowhere. He had little in the way of survival gear, no tent, only a shovel and some dried foodstuffs. A water canteen and first aid kit. *If* he found Kira, he wasn't even sure he could save her with what he had with him. The storm showed no sign of letting up.

Should I have gone to the granaries first when the dot appeared? Why didn't Mackenzie call me back? He'd put a lot of faith in a tracker chip and app made for children and guaranteed to work only if you were within a mile of the child. And yet, the red dot had glowed all night. Whether she was there was the question. Despair gripped him but he mushed Timber and the other dogs onwards.

His only silver lining in the search was the flat terrain. The dogs weren't risking injury, and they loved running. He could see the red dot coming up fast. His hands ached from gripping the sled handles so tight. The pain in his left shoulder kept him awake when the freezing temperatures might have sent him falling off the sled to sleep in the blizzard.

Timber barked. An excited bark, not a warning, which was a relief. Lukas had no desire to run in to one of those seven polar bears even though he had both his rifle and shotgun slung over his back.

"Whoa, whoa boys." He put his weight back on his heels on the sled. They came to a gradual stop as Timber slowed. The other dogs panted and yipped behind him.

"Lay." He waited till the team dropped to their bellies in the snow, their tongues lolling and eyes bright as he shone his battery-operated lantern on them. The red dot was right on top of them. He peered around in a circle, the snow whipping across in front of him from the west. Deep black surrounded him except for the lit snow shining in the beam of his lantern. From what he could see, the snow swept easterly over the tundra in undulated waves like sand in the desert. Except for one hillock sprouting up in a crooked bump.

With his heart in his throat, he told the dogs, "stay put," and left the sled. His boots sank in the snow, but he plowed through it to the mound, raising his lantern as high as he could so as not to miss anything.

Wind-carved snow rivulets wavered across the top of the hump and around a dark hole. With a cry, he dropped to his knees and placed the lantern beside him. He grabbed the frozen snow top with his right hand, pounding through with his fist.

"Kira? Kira?" His balaclava muffled his voice.

Timber whined behind him. He heaved the snow block off, and

there she was, ice particles on her face and hair, her hands together clutching a hunting knife, as if she were praying.

"No! No, no, no... Kira, wake up! Kira, you've got to wake up, sweetheart."

He brushed the protecting snow off her, pulling her upright against him. Her eyes were closed, and her mouth fell open, her head lolling backwards.

"Kira, it's me, it's Lukas. Wake up."

He pulled up his balaclava and put his cheek against her lips. He could feel the faintest breath warm on his skin. "Yes, that's it, breathe. Breathe!"

He rubbed her arms and across her back, up and down, trying to raise a response in her. He kissed her lips, cheeks, eyelids as he tried to warm her up.

"Kira, we've got to get you warm, okay? Hang on..."

Lukas zipped up her jacket. "Timber, come!" He looked over his shoulder as the huge black and white husky came trotting towards him bringing the team along behind.

"Ho! Good dogs, good dogs. Stay." He ruffled Timber's fur around his neck and stood. Hanging onto the team's harness for safety, he crept along till he reached the pack of equipment he'd attached to the sled, including the shovel. With numb fingers, he struggled to cut the nylon ties around Kira's wrists. Then he brought the equipment pack back to the hollow where she lay.

"Circle!" he commanded the team. "Circle!" The dogs followed Timber into the crevasse in the snow Kira had made. Lukas grabbed the shovel and shifted snow to enlarge the area, molding a higher wall around them. He packed the snow down hard with the shovel to surround them and used his gloves to smooth the inside walls. Then he cut a couple of blocks from the snow to rest across the top and climbed back in.

All eight dogs huddled around them, piled on top of each other, nose to tail. Timber lay beside Lukas, his large head resting on Lukas's thigh. Their warmth seeped into Lukas, and he could feel Kira's body becoming warm beside him. He'd tucked his smaller dogs, Tessa and Magnus, behind her. He clicked on his battery lantern for a moment to check her color and breathing.

She rested comfortably against his right shoulder. Her fingers were likely frostbitten. He pulled a pair of mitts on her hands. Her breath rose, regular and even. Although she hadn't regained consciousness, he prayed the warmth from the dog's bodies would be enough to bring her core temp to normal. And he prayed for one more chance to love her and never have to leave her again.

Kira smelled wet dog. Earthy, tangy, unmistakable wet dog. She couldn't move because her arms were pressed tight to her sides and a heavy weight surrounded her. She jerked awake. Her face lay against warm skin. That didn't mesh with her last memory of Jonah's dreadful, angry face shining in his truck headlights. She gasped as the wet nose of an animal grazed her cheek.

"You're okay, Kira," Lukas murmured. "You're all right now."

"Lukas?" It came out in a croak. She tried to shift backwards, but something large and unmoving behind her held her in position.

"Kira! You're awake." Lukas squeezed her so hard she coughed, which led to choking, which led to the dogs whining and yipping.

"Where are we?"

"We're in a snow shelter somewhere in the Wildlife Management Area," he said.

"The storm... is it morning?" She croaked again.

"It's still night. I don't know what time it is. My phone's attached to the sled outside."

"How did you find me out here?"

"Remember when you were playing with Sophie and I put that "Little Lamb" tracker chip in your boot?" She nodded. "I forgot to take it out." He rested his chin on the top of her head. "It worked. It worked over a lot bigger distance than one mile."

Kira shivered.

"Are you still cold?"

"No, I'm warm as anything. I'm just... I don't know." She buried her face in the crux of his neck. "What if Jonah comes back?"

Lukas stilled like a rock beside her. "It was him. Eva said she thought it was him."

Kira sniffed. "I'm sorry, Lukas. But he can find us out here."

"He left you out here for dead?" Lukas's voice held an edge she'd never heard before.

She nodded against his neck. "I couldn't get away. Back at the port."

She eased onto her back and Tessa, the black husky mix, crawled onto her chest, licking her face.

"Did he hurt you?"

"Nothing to worry about... I'm alive, that's all that matters." She patted Tessa's wiry fur, even though her hand felt like a piece of wood.

Lukas sat up on his right elbow. In the tight space, he took a minute to maneuver the battery lamp up towards her face. "Nothing to worry about other than your swollen, black eyes and your bruised cheeks that look like they'll be the colour of eggplants in a day or two."

"Settle down," she said. "If we breathe too much, we'll ice up this shelter."

"We're tabling this discussion till we find Corporal Mackenzie."

Kira sighed. "I was kind of hoping he'd find us."

"He will. I left him enough messages." He brushed ice pellets from her hair. "How about some water, and I'll see what I've got to eat." His thumb brushed her lower lip. "Although it might be hard to eat anything with eight dogs piled in here with us."

"They saved us. We should let them eat first."

"Not until you've had water and I get a look at your hands." Lukas shifted until he found the water canteen he'd put to his right side. "You need to get hydrated."

The water was slushy but not frozen. She tried not to gulp it down so she wouldn't get cramps. She shivered.

"Let's see those hands," Lukas said. He removed the mitts. She wasn't about to tell him she had no feeling in them. Her fingers were bone white, not a good sign. She recoiled from the sight. Another hospital visit was in her immediate future. Tessa's body heat comforted her even as the dog's spiky fur tickled her face.

"Maybe I should tuck them under the dog?"

"Excellent idea." He helped her maneuver them under Tessa, who whimpered and lay back on Kira's chest. "Are you comfortable enough?"

"I'm fine, Lukas." She could feel pins and needles running up and down her feet and legs now. Her cheeks and eyes hurt, which was a good sign. "I'll terrify Sophie again if she sees me like this..."

Lukas lay back on his right side with two other dogs at his back and his arm pillowing Kira's head. "Maybe we'll wait till the black eyes go a bit green."

"They're going to get away with it."

"Jonah won't be hard to find."

"No," Kira wiggled her fingers against Tessa's fur, "they're leaving on a plane as soon as the storm lifts. They'll be gone before we can get word to Corporal Mackenzie."

"Who's *they?*"

"Alison Webster, Ian Birchall, Jonah, and Chelsea. They're all in it together. She's dating Birchall's stepson, Avery, and they were the ones shooting at you. At us." She had another involuntary, full-body shiver.

"I can't believe Jonah hurt you. And left you out here. To die."

She could feel Lukas's chest rise and fall rapidly. "Chelsea's the one I fought with—he gave me a knife for protection."

Lukas turned his head to look at her, his gaze furious. "Doesn't count. You have blood on you. Polar bears can smell blood from twenty miles away; you know that..." He turned back to look upwards, trying to get his breathing under control. "He'll answer for it."

"A polar bear passed right by me about fifteen, twenty feet away. It never even slowed down, Lukas." Kira shifted closer to him. "God was watching over me. And I knew you'd find me somehow. I just had to stay alive long enough."

She snuggled against his good shoulder until she felt the pulse in his neck on her cheek. Safe. Safe and warm like their high school sleigh ride.

"Kira?" His warm breath fanned her face. "I don't know if you can ever forgive me, but I was a Class A jerk." He'd turned on his side to look into her eyes.

"I'm the jerk, remember? I'm the one who ran away." Kira closed her eyes for a second. "There's nothing to forgive you for, Lukas."

Lukas huffed a small breath. "I beg to differ. I was pretty selfish. Thought my car was super special compared to my actual *girlfriend*, who was flesh and blood as opposed to metal and gas fumes. Thought my possessions were the most important things in my life compared to what was right in front of me."

"Well, if you put it that way..." Kira's smile shone in the light of the lantern. "You were pretty selfish sometimes."

"Hey, you don't have to agree with me so fast!"

She pushed him in the chest, her laughter a welcome sound after finding her near death.

"You didn't even let me drive that stupid car, even though you taught me to drive stick in it."

"I don't remember that..."

"Uh, yeah, I remember that; control issues much?"

Lukas drew her closer to himself, chuckling. "Control issues admitted and now refined. It's hard to stay in control when you have a busy toddler."

Their breath mingled in light plumes of airy frost. The dogs snuffled beside them and Lukas went to shut off the lantern. "I'm going to try and conserve the batteries. No telling how long we'll be out here."

"No," Kira said. She put her hand on the lantern. "I'm not afraid of the dark, but it might keep the bears away."

"Smart thinking," said Lukas.

They lay in companionable silence.

"Kira Joy Summers, there's something I need to tell you."

She held her breath. His voice sounded deeper, richer than five years ago. It filled the snowy space surrounding them and the dogs. Enveloped them in security and hope.

She let her breath out slowly. "Yes?"

Lukas's fingertips passed over her injured face, leaving warmth and health behind them. He rubbed his thumb along her chin and tipped it up so her lips were closer to his and she could see his eyes.

"I love you. I've never stopped loving you. I don't care about what happened except that it hurt you terribly, and I want to help you if you'll let me. Can we see if we can start over?"

She stared into his eyes. She'd always loved the deep, ice-blue spokes in his irises. He looked almost frightened, as if she might say no.

"Lukas," she reached up to cup his cheek, "just kiss me!"

This time, his lips were familiar. He kissed her thoroughly, like old times. When they came up for air, she gasped, "I love you, too!"

He chuckled and kissed her on the forehead, hugging her close.

She yawned. "Is it safe for me to go to sleep now?"

"I don't think you're hypothermic. You can catch a few winks."

"Mmm-hmm," she murmured against his chest. "I stayed and fought back, Lukas. No more running away."

He brushed another kiss across her hair. "I know, kiddo. No more running away for either of us."

"I'm pressing charges against Derek Straughn when we get out of this mess." Kira snuggled in closer. "And we will bring charges against Avery Scott for killing my brother." She sighed as she dropped off to sleep.

CHAPTER 16
THREE MONTHS LATER

Ruby's Café and Emporium

K ira parked her snowmobile from the ASRC nose out from the snowbank outside Ruby's Café. She'd spent a long day digitizing her DNA data from the fall satellite recordings of the polar bear migrations across northern Manitoba. Her lower back screamed in protest as she climbed off the machine. She throttled it off and left the keys in the ignition. Anyone needing a quick getaway from a roaming bear in the street was welcome to the snowmobile.

Darkness covered the town even though it was just going on 4:00 p.m. She'd agreed to meet Lukas for a quick bite to celebrate the end of her research project. Since their rescue by Corporal Mackenzie and Sarah Thorvald out on the tundra, and the subsequent avalanche of arrests at the airport, she'd overseen the end-of-season wrap-up. She'd been promoted to Science Coordinator and dealt with Global Environmental Services when they came to clean up the frozen hazardous waste. If Michael hadn't died, the dumping wouldn't have been discovered as early on, and who knew what the effects would've been if Webster Technologies had continued dumping all winter long?

She placed her helmet on the seat of the snowmobile and crossed the cutaway through the snowbank to the front door. The new plate-glass window sparkled with multicolored lights even though it was March instead of November. Since the explosion, Ruby had insisted on keeping the lights up because the café hadn't been open for Christmas.

Kira placed her hand flat on the log door frame and waited a beat. Even though it was rebuilt, Ruby's personality imbued it with a sense of home to tourists and those who lived here year round. The welcoming scent of roasted elk and hot homemade bread wafted towards her on entry. While it took a while to get used to eating game, she now appreciated the local "delicacies" of living in the north.

As she unzipped her snowsuit, she realized Lukas was alone at the counter. And he was wearing a suit jacket over his jeans and a shirt and tie. She hadn't seen him wearing a tie since university. He came across the restaurant and swept her in to his arms, hugging her while he swung her around.

"Okay, okay." She laughed. "What's up with the tie? Court isn't for another month."

Lukas set her on her feet and kissed her, his lips warm on her cold ones.

"I felt like dressing up. We're celebrating, are we not?"

She threw her arms around his neck and enjoyed the solid feel of his chest, the warmth of his body. "We are indeed. And are those Ruby's special elk medallions with roasted root veggies and cranberries?"

"Yes, and I believe we have chocolate pecan pie for dessert." His deep blue eyes glinted in the sparkling mini-lights hanging from the ceiling. "Shall we sit?"

He swung her around to a table set with a white linen tablecloth and white china plates edged in gold. Crystal goblets sat at each place, and an arrangement of perky, March daffodils decorated the center of the table.

Kira gasped. "Where did those come from?"

Lukas put his hand on her elbow and steered her over to her seat. Pulling out her chair with a flourish, he said, "I had them flown in. I figured you could use a little southern sunshine."

Kira drew her forefinger along one, brilliant, yellow petal. "They must've cost you a fortune." With a start, she looked around. "And we're the only ones here tonight?"

"I rented the café for the evening. Ruby said she'd be happy to cook a celebration dinner for us."

Kira cocked an eyebrow. "She's losing a ton of business. Lukas, this is wonderful to celebrate my funding, but it's spending way too much money."

"I want you to relax and enjoy the evening, all right?" He reached behind the counter and pointed a remote up at Ruby's stereo system. The soft sounds of her favourite love song wafted into the room. With a bow, Lukas reached for her hand. "May I have this dance, ma chèrie?"

"What's gotten into you?" She laughed as he swung her around and then settled into a slow two-step. "You know how much I love that song."

"I do. But I don't want the song to do all the talking..." He pressed his forehead to hers.

It's okay, you don't have to be afraid. Nothing's wrong this time.

Her heart thrummed against her rib cage. *Nothing to be afraid of...*

"I'm sorry I was so blind back then... Kira." They swayed slower together. His fingers trembled in her hand.

"It's okay, Lukas..."

"No, it's not okay. You should've been my priority, my only concern." He cleared his throat. "You were the love of my life, and I couldn't see what was wrong, right in front of me." A tear fell on her cheek.

"Lukas..."

He turned his head. "Let me finish. I was an idiot, young, immature. I sure wasn't husband material back then." He pulled her close and rested his head on top of hers as they turned in a circle.

She hugged him around the waist, and her throat felt tight.

"Lukas, I was the one who ran away from you, from everyone. I was... so, so angry. And bitter! I hated him and what happened, and I hated God for letting it happen." She started to cry. "I wasn't exactly wife material either."

He pulled a clean tissue from his jacket pocket and handed it to her. Laughing, she dabbed at her eyes. "You came prepared." She threw back her head and looked up at him. "I'm sorry for running, Lukas. I'm sorry I didn't tell you the truth. I'm sorry I didn't trust you."

"Oh babe, it's all right..." He pulled her to him as the song ended.

"I can't believe you remembered my song." She put her hands on his chest and smiled. "I'm starving."

"Sorry." Lukas pointed to the bottle of sparkling white grape juice on the table. "Shall I pour?"

The usual rush of warmth spilled over her cheeks. Her emotions always betrayed her. "Please." She motioned with her hand.

He put his hand on the small of her back and escorted her to the set table, pulling out her chair and seating her.

"I'm glad you're hungry. Ruby's been cooking all day." He brushed another kiss on the top of her hair.

She ran her hands down the thighs of her black dress pants. She wore a red, cashmere sweater he'd given her for Christmas. Every nerve tingled. Eating supper was the last thing on her mind. Lukas's hands, so strong and capable, poured the juice as if it were fine champagne. He uncovered the basket of bread slices and passed her the butter dish with a smile.

"Shall we say the blessing?"

Kira's cheeks heated. Her heart fluttered in her chest.

It's right this time. Oh God, this is what it feels like when it's right.

"Please, you say it."

"Dear Lord, we have much to be thankful for this year. Please bless the hands that prepared this food, and us to Your service. Amen."

"Amen," she echoed. She took a slice of bread and smothered it with butter.

"You know..." Lukas said.

A small figure in hot pink came bursting through the swinging doors to the kitchen. Long, dark blonde hair and pink, wire-rimmed glasses framed Sophie's sweet face. She carried a small, covered, silver, serving tray in both hands and ran up to their table. Ruby followed close behind her.

Huffing, Ruby said, "I'm so sorry, Lukas, she clean got away from me."

With her lips pursed in great concentration, Sophie placed the silver tray on the edge of the table. She grabbed Kira's closest hand and pressed up against Kira in her chair.

Before Lukas could say anything, Sophie said, "'ill you marry us?"

Lukas choked back a cough.

Sophie lifted the cover on the silver tray with a wild flourish. "See? Is so pretty! Is for you! 'ill you marry us?"

Kira held Sophie's hand, stared across the table at Lukas, and laughed all at the same time.

"Lukas?"

"Well, it's not exactly how I planned it, but..."

He stood and came around the table to Sophie. Kneeling beside her, he took the princess-cut diamond ring out of the blue box on the small tray. He took Sophie's hand and Kira's hand in his and said, "Kira, I've always loved you. I'll never stop loving you. Will you marry us?"

Tears spilled down her cheeks even as she laughed. Kira pulled them both to her and kissed them, hugging them as if she'd never let them go. Ruby stood by, drying her eyes with her apron.

"Yes, I'll marry you both. I love you both so much."

And she knew she'd finally run home.

Want more?
Keep reading for a sneak peek at book 2
NORTHERN PROTECTOR

NORTHERN PROTECTOR

CHAPTER ONE

Saturday, August 1
Churchill, Manitoba

Constable Ben Koper pulled his police truck over to the side of the road across from Ruby's Café & Emporium. His first day back at work in nine months, and already he was running late. He slammed the truck into park and stared up and down Kelsey Boulevard, on high alert for any movement between the buildings.

Last November, a polar bear had attacked him in this exact spot. He hadn't been back to Churchill since then. Goose bumps skittered along his arms. Rationally, he knew that bears had been spotted along the coast and probably hadn't made it into town yet. But his anxiety and the acid in his stomach told his brain a polar bear could be anywhere, now that the sea ice had melted.

Ben grabbed his mobile phone with the coffee orders on it and stepped out of his truck, pulling his baseball cap down to his sunglasses. He slammed the truck door and strode to the pavement of Kelsey Boulevard. The rest of the street sat quiet, while Ruby's 6:00 a.m. crowd was hopping with its early morning breakfast specials. He could see people eating at tables through the huge front plate-glass window.

When he hit the middle of the street, his heart sped up, jackhammering in his chest. His feet refused to move past the centre of the road, like he'd struck an invisible wall. Adrenaline shot through his limbs. His vision tunneled into black holes. Sweat poured down his back and gathered on his forehead. He put his right hand on the grip of his service weapon, trying to get some equilibrium. His throat closed, and he leaned over with his hands on his knees. Deep breaths.

Deep, deep breaths. Trying, trying...

Dan Sherman, his therapist, sounded in his head. *"Look for five things around you to centre yourself. Repeat them to yourself. Then count them down one by one."*

Panting, beads of sweat rolled down the right side of his face over his scarred eyebrow and ear. All he could see was the concrete road and small rocks littered about.

There's nothing but the road. Concrete, rocks, concrete, rocks...

He needed five *things.* His boots wouldn't move. He stood hunched over in the middle of the street, trying not to throw up his meagre breakfast. No other objects around; nothing else to see. His feet... he couldn't move his feet.

Running shoes, white and pink running shoes... Where did they come from?

"Ben? Ben," a lilting, female voice broke through his fog. "Are you okay?"

A hand touched his shoulder, his sore right shoulder, and he flinched. Finally. He could move. He reared his head up and collided with the face belonging to the voice.

"Ow." The woman let go of his shoulder and grabbed her nose while he staggered sideways.

"I'm sorry. I'm sorry," he stammered. He reached forward to steady himself with his right hand but dropped his phone on the ground with his other hand. The woman dove for the phone and swiveled around to give it to him.

"Ben, look at me," she ordered. That voice had a familiar ring to it.

Bossy but comforting at the same time. He'd heard it before. "Let me see you without the sunglasses."

He removed them without question, his heart slowing while sweat made his uniform shirt cling to his back. At nearly 6:30 a.m., no less. Or, what time was it now? He was inexcusably late. Not a great impression to make on the new Corporal.

The woman stood in front of him, her dark brown eyes concerned as she held him by his upper arms. He blinked twice and tried to get his tongue to work. Mortification brought a dull red flush to his cheeks. *I should know her... Gah, why won't my stupid brain work?*

She wore purple nursing scrubs with sprigs of pink flowers on them. Her dark brown hair was pulled back into a braided ponytail, but her eyes—they were the deepest brown he'd ever seen. Several gold earrings pierced her right ear, and one gold stud pierced her left. A delicate scrolled flower tattoo peeked out along her left collarbone. And she smelled of fresh citrus. Like a pitcher of lemonade.

All right, he hadn't totally lost his powers of perception. A gorgeous woman had just pulled him out of a full-blown panic attack in the middle of main street. Wonderful. He might as well turn in his badge and gun, drive straight to the airport, and fly home.

"Ben, it's me." She put her hands on her hips. "It's Joy." She looked like she would snap her fingers in his face any second.

He shook his head. Cleared his throat. Wished the pavement would open and swallow him whole. "I remember."

Joy. When the nightmares came rushing in the night from the bear attack, it was *her* voice and the touch of *her* hands on him as she bound up his shoulder that he remembered. And her scent—that was a great memory—citrusy and fruity after the horror of the bear's mouth and its rancid smell. She had bent over him, bandaging his head with gauze as they tried to save his right ear for the plastic surgeon.

Yes, it was all coming back to him now.

"I'm sorry. Did I hurt you?" *Lord, just beam me a hundred miles away from here, right now. This is not how I wanted to meet her again.*

"No, of course not. How are you?" She touched his forearm lightly.

"I mean really, how are you? You—didn't text me what flight you were coming in on."

"Sorry. I got it last minute." There. At least his voice wasn't shaking like his knees were. Shaking like a trembling foal.

"Great." She took a step back as if realizing she was in his personal space. "I'm so glad... you're back. Most people would never have come up here again after what you went through."

His right shoulder grated in its socket when he put his hand on his service weapon again. That grounded him. Although, he wasn't sure hanging on to his gun was what his therapist had in mind when he said to find objects to fixate on during a panic attack. Time to pop another pain pill, but not with Joy in sight.

"Thanks. I don't blame the bear. He was just being a bear." *Wow. Quit while you're ahead. She's more stunning in person than her texts ever let on.*

"Mommy. I'm gonna be late for day care."

A small, dark head with long hair poked out of the turquoise car parked in front of Ruby's. The child waved at them. "C'mon, Mommy."

"Perfect timing," Joy said under her breath.

"Excuse me?"

"Nothing, never mind," she said. "You sure you're okay? You're not feeling faint or anything?"

Ben took a deep breath, finally. "I'm good. Thanks for checking. Don't know what happened there." He put his sunglasses back on. Small comfort, but a mask all the same.

Joy gave him a slanted look. "Are you going off shift or just going on?"

"Going on, and I'm late. I'm supposed to be bringing in coffee for the guys and a round of Ruby's cupcakes."

"Okay, well, I won't keep you," she said, then started walking back towards Ruby's and her car. The little girl was hanging out the front window of the car from her waist. "Emberlyn Marie Gallagher. Sit back in that car this instant."

A flash of mischief shot through deep brown eyes that were a clone of her mother's as the little girl's face broke into a brilliant smile, and she laughed. Joy kissed the child's upturned face and reached through the open car window to help her back into the front seat.

"I guess I'd better get her over to day care."

"Are you going on shift or coming off?" parroted Ben. *Please don't leave yet.*

"Just going back on a double shift in the ER. Mom had her for the night, so now it's time for day care."

"A double? Is that normal?" *You sound like an overeager teenager. Knock it off.*

Her laugh made his stomach flip. *Yep, definitely feeling like an overeager teenager.*

Joy headed around her car and opened the driver's door. She cocked her head to the side.

"You're going to be fine, Ben." Her smile shone as radiantly as the sunrise. She jumped into her car and slammed the door.

He stood at the bottom of the café steps and watched them drive away. His right shoulder throbbed. It still throbbed every day. He'd lied to his physiotherapist because his short-term disability was up. If he couldn't get back to work, he'd have to quit The Job. He had nothing else *but* The Job. Not being a cop wasn't an option.

"You're going to be fine, Ben."

From your lips to God's ear, Joy Gallagher.

He headed up the steps and yanked open the door. The sweet aroma of baked goods and coffee teased his nose as it welcomed him into the café. Maybe he imagined it, but people seemed to stop talking, especially over at the "gossip" table in the far right corner. He caught the furtive glances, eyes cutting away, and feet rustling under the tables. Was it how he looked? The uniform ball cap didn't cover his ear, but it did cover his right eyebrow and forehead.

"Hey," he said to the air in general. He nodded towards the right and left and then walked up to the counter. Mercifully, people began speaking in low tones again, the sound washing over him like a balm.

He'd expected people to react to his scars when he came back to work, which was why he flew up yesterday to minimize the contact.

Simon Thatcher and Lukas Tanner sat at a table to the left of the front counter. Lukas jumped up and grabbed Ben's right hand, shaking it for all he was worth.

"Hey, why didn't you phone me? It's great to see you."

Ben swallowed his wince as Lukas clapped him on the right shoulder. "Sorry, just got the word I could get back to work, so I flew in last night. I don't even have groceries." He nodded at Simon, who raised his coffee mug in a salute. "It's great to see you, too. How was the wedding?"

Lukas's grin could've powered the town for a month. "I was sorry you had to miss it. We honeymooned in Florida and took Sophie with us. She loved every second of it."

"That's good, buddy. Real good."

"I'm so glad you're back. Kira's going to want to have you over for supper."

"Yeah, I'll let you know what my schedule is... once I know."

"Hey there, what can I get you?" asked a young teenaged girl behind the counter. She looked fresh as the sunrise, all blonde and blue-eyed perfection. No sign of recognition, and he didn't know her name, either.

"Can I get a half dozen chocolate cupcakes and a half dozen red velvet ones, please?" He smiled back at the girl. "And two double-double coffees, one black, and one cream, no sugar."

"Absolutely." She threw together a paper box and reached into the glass-topped counter to load it up with the cupcakes. "Zoe, can you grab that coffee order for me?"

"Got it," yelled Zoe from the back.

"Don't be a stranger, okay?" said Lukas.

"No worries. I'll text you."

Lukas went back to his table and started talking quietly with Simon.

Ben rocked on his heels, his hand on his service weapon without realizing it. He glanced up to the left at the slanted mirror that Ruby had installed over the cash register. It also showed the front doors. No one was behind him. His unease rippled up from the base of his spine. He and his therapist had talked about this—that feeling of something crawling up his back. Of something waiting behind him. What it was, he didn't know. But the feeling made him sick in the pit of his stomach.

He tried another deep breath, then smiled a crooked smile at the blonde girl when he paid for his coffees and cupcakes. He'd never felt like he had a target on his back in uniform before. Zoe brought him a cardboard tray with the coffee cups in it, and he grasped it for dear life. With the cupcake box in his other hand, he nodded again at the girls but couldn't manage to get a word out.

Eight long steps between the counter and the front door. He pushed through the plate glass door on the right, into the sunshine of a cloudless day. Now to get back across the road to his truck. His heart fluttered in his chest, ramping up like hummingbird wings. This wasn't happening. *It couldn't be happening.* He could do this, and without Joy Gallagher or anyone else.

The thought of the white pills waiting for him in the glove box of his truck steadied his nerves. This was his last coffee run—from now on, he'd bring a travel mug and to heck with the cupcakes. He made it to his truck and jumped inside as if a bear was after him, sending the coffees sideways and causing them to leak from their lids. *Nice. Coffee dripping everywhere, you idiot.* Heart pounding, he tossed back two pain pills, swallowing them dry.

If only she could see you now. He shoved the thought of Joy's bottom-less brown eyes away and started the truck. *The Job.* It's who he was, what he was, and all he had in the world. *Focus on that, buddy,* he told himself as he pulled onto the road. *Focus on that.*

"What's wrong with the policeman, Mommy?"

"Nothing, honey. I just had to talk to him," said Joy. She hung a right to go north and then a left at the Town Centre.

Her ancient two-door sedan had nearly 110,000 kilometers on it. Up here, everyone drove their vehicles into the ground. The only places to go were around town, out to the airport, or along the coast twenty-three kilometers to the Arctic Studies Research Centre. She'd gotten this car from her parents when she was sixteen, but it was already well used then.

She helped Emberlyn out of her car seat and let her skip along the sidewalk towards the main doors. Her princess backpack bounced on her thin shoulders when she hopscotched on invisible squares before hitting the automatic door opener with the flat of her palm.

"His ear looks ugly," said Emberlyn. They entered the air-conditioned building that housed every important business for the town. The Town Complex stretched for five city blocks along the shoreline.

Joy worked in the Health Centre here and loved the fact that she could leave Emberlyn in the Little Tots Day Care because it had extended hours for shift workers. They walked past the library and down the hallway towards the indoor play area, where young moms and their little kids congregated on days of inclement weather.

That's because he got mauled by the polar bear last winter," she said as she held the inner door open for her daughter. "Don't say that to anyone. I'm sure Constable Koper's self-conscious about it."

"I won't." Emberlyn skipped into the day care foyer, her light-up runners flashing pink and purple lights. "Can he hear out of it?"

"I'm sure he can, or he wouldn't be back at work." She stood by while Emberlyn hung up her backpack in her cubby and toed off her runners. Fatigue washed over her. Her Saturday overnight shift had been busier than usual. A fight at the Legion and two domestics. It made it harder when she knew the victims.

"Okay." Emberlyn shrugged and reached up for a quick hug and kiss. "Love you, Mommy."

"Love you too, baby." She squeezed her daughter tightly. It was so hard to leave her in the care of others besides herself or her own mother. She straightened as Shannon appeared.

"Hey, Emberlyn. Are you ready for breakfast, or did you eat at Gramma's house?"

"We had chocolate chip pancakes," said Emberlyn, beaming.

"Gramma let me pour the pancake batter because I'm six now and big enough." She clutched her princess doll to her side. "I can help you make breakfast."

Shannon laughed. "Well, aren't you wide awake this morning. Sure, you can help make breakfast for the little kids." She took Emberlyn by the hand and smiled at Joy. "Looks like you could use a decent sleep. Rough shift?"

Joy shrugged. "Eh, rough enough. I didn't get much sleep before I went on." She ruffled Emberlyn's hair. "I'll be back to get her by 5 p.m. Bye, squirt."

"Bye, Mommy."

Joy watched the two of them disappear into the kitchen, then headed back out to her car. Every part of her ached from being on the run all shift. But it was the middle of summer, which meant staff shortages from holidays. After this next shift, she'd be able to collapse into sleep while her mom took Emberlyn for the night again.

Driving back down the hill, she remembered the feel of Ben's hard shoulder under her hand. Something about it wasn't right. She touched her throbbing nose ruefully. Served her right for scaring the poor man. He'd been having a full-blown panic attack. She hoped for his sake, he'd had some therapy back in Winnipeg. No one here expected to see him again after his close brush with death.

They'd stabilized him with two blood transfusions and a quick surgery to put his shoulder back in place, before helicoptering him down to the Health Sciences Centre in Winnipeg for proper reconstructive surgery. Her boss, Dr. Will Stedman knew the plastic surgeon who'd reattached Ben's right ear and fixed the scarring on his face and right eyebrow.

Emberlyn was right. His damaged ear was noticeable—but only because as a police officer, he had to wear his hair short, and it was uncovered. Kudos to him for being brave enough not to care what people thought of his looks. And for coming back here where he was injured in the first place. She didn't know if she would've had the guts to go through with it. On the other hand, her return to Churchill had taken a different kind of courage.

She wheeled around the corner of the building into the Health Centre staff parking. Time to grab another coffee and get back to work.

Want more?
Order your copy of Northern Protector on Amazon
or at anaiahpress.com

CPSIA information can be obtained
at www.ICGtesting.com
Printed in the USA
LVHW030518030322
712268LV00005B/27/J